Victims of Violence

VICTIMS OF VIOLENCE

Janie Bolitho

Constable · London

First published in Great Britain 1999
by Constable & Company Limited
3 The Lanchesters, 162 Fulham Palace Road
London W6 9ER

Copyright © Janie Bolitho 1999

The right of Janie Bolitho to be
identified as the author of this work
has been asserted by her in accordance
with the Copyright, Designs and Patents Act 1988

ISBN 0 094 79440 5

Set in Palatino 10 pt by
SetSystems Ltd, Saffron Walden, Essex
Printed and bound in Great Britain
by MPG Books Ltd, Bodmin, Cornwall

A CIP catalogue record for this book
is available from the British Library

For the players, management and supporters of
Plymouth Parkway FC

1

Elizabeth Smith lived in a nondescript red-brick house. It was indistinguishable from its neighbours. An oblong of lawn and a low hedge separated each property from the street. Opposite her were the high walls, also built of red brick, of what had once been one of the small hospitals which had served Rickenham Green. Since the vast concrete and glass edifice of Rickenham General had been erected in a suitably inconvenient location several miles from the town centre, St Luke's Hospital had become a repository for unwanted elderly members of the family.

From her silent vigils at her window Elizabeth saw few visitors pull in through the ever-open wrought-iron gates. She wondered if she might end up there herself in the not too distant future.

Her life was reflected in her surroundings: routine, dull and unexciting. Her childhood had not been exactly miserable but neither had it been fun. Christened after the then Princess Elizabeth, she had been brought up to emulate the way in which her mother believed the future Queen would behave.

'Princess Elizabeth would never say that,' or 'Princess Elizabeth wouldn't do that.' How those phrases still reverberated in her head. As a young girl Elizabeth had often wondered how the Royal Family managed to survive with so many restrictions upon their lives. It all amounted to the same thing; she was expected to show decorum, to behave like a lady and to display good manners at all times. Elizabeth Smith had been stifled as a child and afraid to live as an adult. School had been followed by a childless marriage of thirty years to Henry.

One evening when they were seated at the dining-table in the window of the lounge he had tucked his white linen napkin into the collar of his shirt, an act which made Elizabeth cringe every time they ate together, opened his mouth to speak then slumped neatly on to the floor. She looked at him in surprise and half smiled. There was no mess, no noise; he had, she supposed, died with decorum. That was ten years ago and she didn't miss him because there was nothing to miss. They had had no interests either in common or separately and the sexual side of their marriage had waned years ago. In fact, she thought, as she looked out at the dismal sky, she had hardly known Henry.

A regular passer-by might well have mistaken Elizabeth for one of those women who twitch at net curtains, not that she had any, but they would have been wrong. She had no interest in her fellow human beings other than in the wrong they might do her. She was terrified of the modern world, from what she learned via the media rather than from experience. Youngsters, no matter how unaggressive, frightened her, and worse still were the football supporters.

Her house, and the others in the row, backed on to the ground of Rickenham Athletic with only an access path in between. When there was a match the cheering and shouting carried clearly from the stands. To Elizabeth it was the sound of the jungle, primitive and incomprehensible.

Once, when there had been an evening kick-off, she had gone to the kitchen to make tea, not bothering to put on the lights because the floodlights illuminated the back of the house and part of the garden. She had stood, hand to her mouth, frozen in horror. At the bottom of the garden a man stood urinating on to a flower bed. Too shocked to move, she had watched until he had zipped up his trousers and left, shutting the gate behind him.

On another occasion, before an afternoon kick-off, some youths had swaggered past, drinking from bottles, some of which they had thrown into her front garden. Her fear of what might have happened to her had she challenged any of these individuals was greater than her outrage, so she did nothing.

Now, on a bitter December afternoon, she stood at the lounge window watching the spectators making their way to the football ground. The crowds were small, never more than five or six hundred, but many of them used Alma Road as a short-cut because, midway, the row was broken by a lane leading to the access path. Here was the turnstile which led to the side of the ground favoured by the home crowd. It was a quarter to three and she could already hear the music from the loudspeakers.

At ten past three she sighed with relief, drew her lilac cardigan closely to her thin body and went to make a cup of tea. Then she took up her knitting and listened to Radio 4.

8

At four fifty her vigil was resumed. Most of the crowd went straight home, especially fathers with children, but some stayed on to drink in the clubhouse which meant she could not relax until six thirty when the back turnstile was locked up. After that anyone else had to leave by the main entrance which led to Bradley Road.

She heard a muffled voice over the tannoy then one or two people drifted past. They were followed by larger groups, many in black and white scarves and bobble hats which were the colours of Rickenham Athletic. One young man with dyed yellow hair and a ring through his nose glanced her way. He grinned and waved. At first Elizabeth thought he had raised his hand to aim some sort of missile before she realised that most people were smiling. They must have won, she thought, and he probably thinks I care. She did not wave back. To return his salute would have amounted to a breach of etiquette.

The streetlights had been on for some time, as had the white globes on the gateposts of St Luke's Hospital which were just to the left of her window. She could see quite clearly and only needed glasses for reading.

She sighed, wishing time away, waiting for six thirty. At twenty past, two couples strolled by and one of the men started punching the air and singing 'We're on our way to Wembley'. Elizabeth had no idea what he could mean. She had never heard of the FA Vase and was unaware that Rickenham Athletic had won all their matches in it so far.

Silence at last. She was able to hear the whoosh of the gas boiler which worked on a thermostat and fired the central heating and the sombre ticking of the clock encased in a wooden frame which sat on the dresser. Now she was free to prepare her evening meal and watch a bit of television. There was no need to draw the curtains. Except on match days the road was little used; apart from the occasional visitor to St Luke's Hospital, the only people likely to pass were fellow residents and they mostly used their cars.

The smoked haddock she had bought for supper would take no time to cook. She buttered some bread to go with it. Carrying the tray back to the lounge she saw the elongated shadow of someone coming up the road spread itself across the hospital wall. Frowning she went to investigate. At least someone round here knows what their feet are for, she thought, as a man came into view.

'Good heavens!' She could not help the exclamation. There was a second shadow, it was most uncanny. The second man wore a football scarf, one of the opponents, she thought knowledgeably, because it was not black and white. For this reason only did she go closer to the window and peer out. An away supporter, if his team had lost and he had drink inside him, might be capable of anything.

Something was happening. She heard some muffled noises and the sound of something metal being dropped. This was followed by the echo of running footsteps. This time the shadow followed, rather than preceded, the man who was racing back down the road the way he had come.

Elizabeth Smith made the first brave move of her life. She left the steaming haddock on the table and went to the front door and opened it. She took the few steps to the gate and peered in both directions. Huddled against the wall by the old hospital was a man; the second man. She knew it was him because he was wearing the football scarf.

She crossed the road. Her mouth was dry and she was trembling violently, partly out of fear but mainly because she had no coat and the temperature had dropped below freezing. Timidly, she leaned forward, fearful that he might come to and attack her. She straightened and looked around. There was no one else in sight. Some houses showed only blank windows, others had drawn curtains and on the side of the road where she stood there was nothing but the high hospital wall.

Elizabeth staggered a few yards, balanced herself with one hand against the ivy-covered bricks and vomited on to the tarmac.

He could not attack her, of course. From the moment she had seen the blood oozing from his nose and the sticky mess of his dark hair she had known he was dead. Even as she forced her legs to work and lurched over the road to telephone for an ambulance and the police she hoped that none of her neighbours had seen her being sick. It would have been so humiliating. Ladies were not supposed to show revulsion – it was considered to be bad-mannered.

Killing someone isn't very mannerly, either, Elizabeth managed to think as she hit the button embossed with the number nine three times.

Moira Roper was coming to the end of another term at night school. It had been a struggle but she was finally getting to grips with the law course she had undertaken. However, with Ian on leave and her daytime job in the office of the car showrooms, she was finding it impossible to study as much as she wished.

Ian had decided to spend his leave at home, which had not surprised Moira. He only took holidays abroad for her sake and besides, as he had pointed out, Moira had used up her annual allocation. He certainly wasn't going off somewhere alone. 'I'm simply going to relax; to sleep late, watch daytime television and go for a drink at lunchtime if I feel like it. I'll be ready to face Mark when he comes home for Christmas then,' he had told her with a grin. What had surprised her was how much he was enjoying his time off. Over the years he had rarely managed to conceal the boredom he felt after a few days, even if they went abroad. She had believed, from recent throw-away comments, that he was beginning to feel his age and was not sorry to have the opportunity to slow down a bit. How wrong she had been. Indeed, on Monday, his first day off, he had slept late and spent a lazy day with the papers and a book. But on Tuesday morning he had got up at the same time as Moira and asked for a lift into town. 'What's wrong with your car?' she had asked, startled to see him up and dressed so early.

'Nothing. I intend walking back. It'll do me good.'

'But why so early?'

'Ah, I've got things to do.'

And when she returned from work on Tuesday evening she had stood in the kitchen doorway unable to believe what she thought she could smell. Paint. Yes, definitely paint. 'Ian?' she had called out tentatively. Any decorating had always been done by herself. In all the years she had known him her husband had never picked up a paintbrush nor shown the slightest interest in improving their home.

Ian was in Mark's old room. Moira gaped at the paint-splattered man. There were spots of white gloss in his hair. 'I don't believe it!' she said, shaking her head. The window was wide open, letting in the chilly evening air, and the lampshade had been removed to allow the bulb to cast an unshadowed light. The single bed had been pulled to the middle of the room and was shrouded in an old sheet and the skirting boards, windowsill and window frame were a gleaming white. 'Where's the carpet?

'I took it up and rolled it. It's in our room for the moment.'

'I have to admit, if you decide to do something you don't do it by halves.' Moira usually spread newspaper on the floor to catch the drips.

'Well, what do you think?'

'I don't know what to say. It's perfect.'

'Come with me.' He led her to the hall cupboard. 'Now, what do you think of this?' Proudly, he unrolled a few feet of wallpaper.

'Oh, Ian, it's the sort of thing I'd have chosen myself. But I won't have time to do it before Mark gets home.'

'You won't need to. I'm going to have a bash myself.'

'But, Ian, you need to match the pattern.'

'I know that. I had a long chat with the bloke in the shop.'

'And the carpet?'

'Ah, well, I'm hoping that'll go back as easily as it came up. If not, I'll get someone in.'

And for the next two days Ian had concentrated his efforts on papering, continuing until into the evening. It was a medium-sized room but it was his first attempt and most of the lengths had to be rehung more than once before he considered them to be perfect. Moira listened to the cursing and grumbling with amusement but did not interfere because she knew that he was enjoying himself. And she had been forbidden entry until the room was complete.

Moira's next shock came on Friday morning when she awoke to the sound of hammering coming from Mark's room where the carpet was being relaid. 'Ian, it's seven thirty,' she said loudly to the closed door.

'I know. I don't think this'll take too long.'

The banging and crashing had ceased by the time she returned from work, glad of the weekend ahead of her. Ian was in the sitting-room reading the paper. He grinned when he saw her. 'Now, tell me what you think.' Taking her hand he led her upstairs. Moira stared at the room then back at Ian. Tears filled her eyes. He looked so boyish and so proud of himself as he grinned with pleasure. 'It's lovely. It really is. Thank you.' She reached up to kiss him. Never, she told herself, would she mention that two of the lengths did not quite match even though it would irritate her each time she entered the room. For a first attempt it was excellent.

'I thought I might have a go at the bathroom next. It'll be easy compared to this. Just gloss and a new coat of paint up to the tiles. You can choose the colour.'

Moira laughed. 'That's very generous of you.' But the laughter also contained relief. He was not yet ready to tackle new tiles.

It was nine thirty on Saturday morning and they had had a lie-in. Moira was spoiling Ian by cooking a proper breakfast as a reward for his decorating. As she stood by the cooker in faded denims, low-heeled boots and a brightly patterned sweater, her face free of make-up and her fair hair tied back in a pony-tail, Ian thought how fresh she always managed to look and was reminded anew of the gap in their ages. She bent to add halved tomatoes to the bacon and sausages which were sizzling under the grill and he felt a surge of desire as her slim curves were outlined beneath the taut denim. He picked up a tin of beans and smirked. 'Goddammit!' he said a second later. 'Why doesn't this damn thing work?'

Moira smiled. He may have mastered the art of wallpapering but he still couldn't work simple gadgetry. 'Give it to me.' She took the can of baked beans and expertly slotted it beneath the wheel of the wall-mounted tin-opener. With one smooth movement the circle of the lid dropped on to the beans.

They ate in companionable silence until Ian heard the rattle of the letter-box and the thud of the heavily supplemented Saturday paper dropping on to the mat. He went to fetch it. Having discarded the sections neither of them bothered to read, he propped the editorial page against the sauce bottle and glanced at it as he ate. For once Moira did not complain.

They were to spend the day together, a rare occurrence. After breakfast some shopping, but not for essentials – they would treat themselves to something, although Ian had now decided they would also choose the bathroom paint. They'd skip lunch and have a walk somewhere on the coast, rain or shine, and later they were going to the Duke of Clarence for a meal. Ian had already booked a table.

13

'Ian?'

'Mmm?' He did not look up.

'Look, I know shopping isn't your idea of a good time, why don't you go to football instead?'

'What?' He stared at her in surprise. Moira did not mind, had never minded him going to matches, but today had been his idea, a bit of a thank you for the times when work prevented him from seeing her for days.

Moira smiled. 'I mean it. Honestly. We can still eat out tonight.'

Ian reached across the table and squeezed her hand causing her to flinch because her engagement ring had slipped and the stone was trapped between her fingers. 'Sure?'

'Positive.'

'Okay. But we can still have a look around the shops and get the paint first.' He stood and stretched, his arms above his head, his fists balled. Moira looked up at the six feet four inches which comprised her husband and smiled. How easily pleased he was. Maybe she ought to buy herself a Norwich City strip and slip it on whenever a bad mood threatened. She smiled to herself. It would be different from the stereotypical nurse's uniform.

Ian's heavy tread on the stairs was followed by the sound of the shower running. Twenty minutes later he reappeared, clean and shaven and dressed in dark brown casual trousers, a shirt and a crew neck oatmeal jumper. Moira had tidied the kitchen and loaded the dishwasher. They were ready to go out.

By twelve thirty Moira was in possession of a cream silk blouse; Ian's carrier bag contained a pair of new shoes and a tin of the palest apple green paint. He dropped Moira at home then set off immediately, turning to wave to her as she watched him from the front window of their house in Belmont Terrace. It was a miserable, raw, damp day but now their afternoon plans had been cancelled and without the temptation of decent weather to lure her out, it was the perfect opportunity for her to do some studying.

Rickenham Green was in Suffolk but Ian supported Norwich rather than Ipswich. He had once explained why his allegiance was with the Canaries but Moira had forgotten his reasons, just as she instantly forgot the details when he talked her through a game upon his return. Win or lose, he would expound his theories as to why the result stood as it did and how the match ought to have been played. Let them win, she thought, before opening a textbook.

Stopping only for coffee she worked until three thirty when her eyes began to ache. She wondered if she needed to get them tested. Glancing out of the window there was nothing to see but the parked cars which permanently lined the road since nearly every family now possessed more than one. It would be dark soon. She packed away her books and went upstairs to decide what to wear. She selected a long-sleeved fine wool dress and high-heeled shoes. The Duke of Clarence was somewhere to dress up for. Then she had a bath and washed her hair.

Satisfied with her appearance she went downstairs and flicked on the television for the football results. It was better to be prepared. 'Thank goodness,' she sighed as her eyes moved rapidly down the screen to pick out Norwich's score before the broadcaster's sing-song voice announced it.

It took Ian a good hour to get home, a bit longer if the traffic was bad, but their reservation was for eight thirty so there was plenty of time. Moira poured a glass of dry white wine and sat down to read. This time it was a novel, she had had enough of textbooks for one day.

At six forty-five Ian still wasn't home. At seven she began to worry. He had the car, he would not have stopped for a celebratory drink. Pacing the kitchen she wondered why he hadn't rung.

By seven thirty she was frantic. She moved swiftly across the room to switch on the radio for the local news. Perhaps there had been an accident which was blocking the road, or crowd trouble, or extra time. Extra time and penalties, how long would that take? She didn't know exactly why and when this happened, only that it sometimes did. No. Norwich's result had been read out along with the others. The match had finished on time.

The local news had just come on. 'Jarvis Dunstone, MP for Saxborough West, has announced his intention to retire from politics at the next general election,' Moira heard the announcer say. 'So far, no alternative candidates have been proposed.

'And now to sport. Ipswich's match against Nottingham Forest kicks off tomorrow afternoon but, good news for supporters of non-league football, Rickenham Athletic are through to the next round of the FA Vase after a resounding five-nil victory over the northern side, Gravesby Wanderers.

15

'And we've just received some late news. The body of a man was discovered in Alma Road, Rickenham Green, earlier this evening. It is thought he was beaten to death although the police are refusing to comment until they have more information. He is believed to be a Norwich City supporter but no further details will be released until the relatives have been informed.

'Now here is the weather forecast read by . . .'

But Moira wasn't listening. Her legs had given way and she sank on to a kitchen chair. Ian, was her initial reaction, but only because he made such a thing about supporting the Canaries. To listen to him anyone would think he was the only Norwich City fan in Rickenham.

In all their married life, especially when Ian had worked a beat, she had expected almost daily to hear that he had been killed in the line of duty. Impossible to imagine him dying in these circumstances. But he was late, very late, and he had not phoned. Anxiety activated her imagination.

It can't be Ian, she decided with a sigh. But it would be typical of him to have somehow become involved, to have picked up the news via his car radio and gone straight to the scene, forgetting their arrangements for the evening. But the dread remained, a heavy feeling in her guts. So why hadn't he rung her? Because work comes first, as always, she thought, angry now. No one had telephoned, no police officer had come to her door, it couldn't be Ian. But what if it was? What if just this once he had managed to be in the wrong place at the wrong time? Ian had often told her that no one believes terrible things happen to people they know, until it does happen, and then they take some convincing.

She went to the coat hooks in the hall. His scarf wasn't there, although he often kept it in the boot of the car.

It was the not knowing which made her cry, the emotional swings between fury that he could let her down today, of all days, when she had given up her afternoon so he could go to football, and the fear of the unthinkable. Tears landed on the cream wool of her dress and ruined her make-up as she wiped them away.

She returned to the kitchen to listen for any further bulletins. No more details would be given until the relatives had been informed, the earlier one had said. Ian always carried his identity, they would know at once who he was.

'Unless he was mugged and his pockets emptied,' a voice whispered in her head. But if it was murder senior police officers would have gone to the scene, they would have recognised Ian.

Moira clutched the back of a kitchen chair for support. Expecting the telephone or the front doorbell to ring she jumped when the back door swung open. 'My God! You bastard.' Now she knew he was safe, anger came to the fore.

'Moira?' Ian's mouth dropped open. 'Moira, what is it? What's happened?' He advanced quickly towards her and enveloped her in his arms. She could feel the damp coldness of his coat even though he had presumably only walked the short distance from the car around the side of the house. Its fabric was rough against her face as she felt the prickle of tears again.

'I thought . . . I don't know what I thought. But I was beginning to think you were dead,' she finally managed to stutter.

'Because I was late?' Ian was incredulous. Throughout their married life he had been late frequently, although he had mostly managed to warn her of the possibility. Moira had understood what his work entailed. Surely she wasn't upset because he had gone to the match after all? But it was so unlike her to be this upset.

'No. Not just because you were late but because you didn't ring me and because I heard on the news that a Norwich City supporter was killed.'

'What?'

She nodded. 'Not long ago. It came up in a news flash.'

Ian frowned. He hadn't spotted any trouble inside or outside the ground and there certainly hadn't been a larger police presence than usual when he had left.

'It was here, in Rickenham,' Moira added. 'Where's Alma Road?'

Ian stroked her head as she blew her nose noisily, gratified and touched that she cared so much.

'Anyway, where were you? And why on earth didn't you telephone?'

'I was just leaving Norwich when a lorry shed its load. After a hell of a wait someone finally organised a system of one-lane traffic. I rang from the car-phone several times but there was no answer.'

'But I was – ' She stopped; the fingertips of both hands flew to

17

her lips as she began to laugh, half in earnest, half hysterically. 'Oh, no! Oh, Ian, what a fool I've been.'

He waited, arms folded, one eyebrow raised in a question.

Moira shook her head in disbelief. 'This morning you were sleeping so soundly that I pulled out the phone jack in case my mother rang early. I forgot to plug it back in again.' Had she needed to use the phone herself none of this would have happened. It was a lesson learned.

Ian grinned, glad that he wasn't to bear one hundred per cent of the blame. 'At least I know you care. Come on, look at the time, we'd better get moving.'

'My face . . .'

'It's lovely.'

'No, Ian, I can't, not like this. Give me five minutes?'

'All right but I'll ring for a taxi then we'll still have time for a drink first.' He did so whilst Moira repaired the ravages of tears and twenty minutes later they were seated in the bar of the Duke of Clarence where Moira shunned her usual white wine in favour of a reviving cocktail. Ian stuck to a pint of the local Adnams bitter.

As Moira studied the dresses of the other women Ian wondered at the complexities of life. How many Norwich City supporters were there in Rickenham? And how many would have travelled to the match and would therefore be wearing the team's colours? Ian assumed this was the way in which the victim had been identified as a supporter. There would have been time for him to get home from the game, a good hour and a half, as long as he hadn't parked in the vicinity of the lorry which had shed its load, or if he had taken the train. And how ironic to be found only yards from another ground, that of Rickenham Athletic. Presumably he lived nearby. He looked up and smiled at his wife; he was on leave, it was someone else's problem.

The smile faded. During the match and the minor drama which had unfolded upon his return he had been able to forget that Detective Sergeant, now Detective Inspector, Barry Swan had been transferred, at his own request, to Gloucester. He and Lucy and baby Martin were no longer a part of their lives. How he would miss him; the long discussions, the drinks after work, the socialising with their wives. They had been a team. Ian had had no idea his leaving would hurt so much.

An immaculate waiter cast a shadow over Ian. 'Menus, sir, and the wine list.' He handed Moira one and Ian two leather-bound folders. 'Your table's ready whenever you are, sir.'

'Thank you.' Ian decided that for Moira's sake he would not think about Barry that evening. Having witnessed her reaction earlier he knew how very lucky he was and that missing Barry was only a fraction of what he would feel if Moira were no longer around.

2

Detective Sergeant Markham, known to everyone simply as Markham, was of over average height although nowhere near as tall as the chief inspector. He was well built and his preference for walking rather than driving kept him fit. The firm, uncompromising features and short-cropped hair were not deceptive, they summed up Markham's character which was why, although he was not disliked, he was not someone whom colleagues confided in or chose to add to their circle of friends. They saw him for what he was: a loner who preferred it that way. And he was a good detective, if a little unusual in his methods.

For the past couple of days Markham had been wondering about young Richie Andrews whom he had seen several times recently. He was surprised he had stayed in Rickenham Green after what had happened. No previous, he recalled, and no other crimes asked to be taken into account when he was sentenced. He had read the social report. Andrews' parents were wealthy. Had the crime been a one-off? A rich kid's idea of fun or a frustrated kick at the establishment? Markham could not make him out, yet he had felt some kind of empathy with him, a recognition of something in common.

So why's he still here and what's he doing? Markham was thinking. PC Cotton walked that beat. He would have a word with him and ask him to keep an eye on Richie Andrews.

It was five thirty on Saturday afternoon and he was sitting in the general office at the Rickenham Green police headquarters wondering how to spend the evening. It was dark and miserable outside, neither raining nor dry, just a cold dampness that might have been depressing to anyone who noticed the weather. Not so Markham. He did not know why this was, why he was so uninterested in such things. For some reason the day of the funeral came into his mind. It was almost a year ago when Martin Cooper, Richie's best friend, had been buried and, later the same day, young Vaughan had been cremated. Markham's instinct told him that Richie Andrews had remained in Rickenham for a purpose. He decided to get out the file and reread it, and he'd take another look at what the social worker had to say. Sometimes, he thought with a wry grin, they came out with something worth listening to.

Detective Chief Inspector Ian Roper, usually referred to as the Chief, was on leave. Inspector Short, newly seconded to their team, had been made up temporarily to Ian's rank in his absence. So far he had had little to do, which was just as well as he seemed disinclined to shift from behind his desk.

When the call came regarding an incident in Alma Road Short was nowhere to be found. It's me then, I suppose, Markham thought, realising he was the most senior detective available. Short would have to join him later.

Having stared unblinkingly at the body of the youngish man sprawled on the ground with his head bashed in, Markham followed the procedure for the initial stages of a murder inquiry. Superintendent Thorne had been contacted and had given the go ahead.

The victim was surprisngly well dressed for someone who had been to a football match but perhaps he had been a guest in a box or was some sort of club official. Soon he would know. Soon he would know more about this man than his own mother did.

Almost an hour later he ducked out of the tent which had been erected over the body and glanced across at 11 Alma Road. Odd and even numbers were on the same side as the hospital pre-dated the houses. Lights were blazing in Elizabeth Smith's house, the downstairs curtains undrawn. Markham summed up the neighbourhood. It was a quiet, mind-your-own-business sort of street. There would be few pedestrians except when the football was on and this evening there would have been a hiatus from the time the last spectators left the ground until the discovery of the body. Now, despite the arctic conditions, people were huddled on doorsteps, their coats on, making no bones about their curiosity. Not that there was anything to see now, not unless arc lights and cold policemen with their squawking radios counted.

The ambulance had been sent on its way as soon as it had arrived. There was nothing the paramedics could do for this Norwich City supporter. They were waiting for the Home Office pathologist who would perform his ritualistic tasks while the rest of the team stood around impatient for him to finish. No one knew how long it would take for him to arrive. No Doc Harris, for this one. This was no elderly person who had been found in bed whom the police surgeon on duty could certify as having died from natural causes.

Markham shoved his hands in the pockets of his jeans and sighed. A woman had taken it into her head to cross the road to his side despite a uniformed officer stationed there to prevent this. 'Madam, you can't – ' he began warningly.

'I just wanted to ask if anyone wanted some tea. You must all be freezing.'

'No, thanks, not for me. Stay there while I ask the others.' He looked back over his shoulder to make sure she complied and stuck his head in the tent. It was bitterly cold but Markham seemed not to notice. Nevertheless he understood that his fellow officers, hanging around until it was their turn to take part in events, were probably numb with cold and dying for a cup of tea. Markham returned to the woman. 'Can you run to nine cups?'

Her eyes lit up. She was, after all, to be part of the carnival. 'Yes. I've got disposable ones we use for picnics in the summer.'

'That's fine. Just hand them to PC Donaldson over there.' Markham indicated a tall, lean man who, beneath the arc lights, looked blue with cold.

Inspector Short was conspicuous by his absence but no one seemed able to locate him. Markham's lip curled in a grin. Short was also a law unto himself but this was really going to land him in it. There was no excuse for being incommunicado whilst on duty. So we're one short, he thought, amused at his own pun. It was time to call on the old dear who had summoned them.

Shoulders hunched, Markham crossed the road and rang the

doorbell. A WPC he did not recognise came to the door. 'How is she?' Markham asked quietly, imagining a trembling figure on the verge of fainting.

'I'm WPC Blount.' The young woman introduced herself and raised her eyebrows. 'Mrs Smith's in here,' she said, loudly enough for the occupant of the house to hear.

Markham shrugged and followed her into the lounge where there was a faint smell of fish. Sitting in an overstuffed armchair, quite at ease, sat a woman he took to be in her late sixties, or possibly a little older. She wore a grey dress, a lilac cardigan and neat grey shoes. Her short hair was carefully but softly permed, not springing tightly from her head in the way favoured by some women her age. Her papery cheeks were pale but she wore subtle pink lipstick and a touch of mascara which showed she had not given up on her appearance. Markham introduced himself.

'How do you do.' Elizabeth held out a hand which Markham took. She had a firm grip. 'Do you know PC Blount? She's asked me to call her Liz. We share the same first name.'

Not the type to require smelling salts, Markham decided, although he had noticed the vomit by the wall not far from the body. Hers, or the victim's, or a drunken Rickenham Athletic supporter's?

Mrs Smith was obviously not too distraught to be questioned. 'I suppose you'd like me to tell you in my own words what I saw?' she said, surprising Markham further. He had no way of knowing this was one of the biggest highlights of the woman's life.

Markham met the eyes of Liz Blount who was about to make them all tea. She grinned as if to say, See what I mean? then left the room. He watched her go, admiring the neat behind and slim waist in the uniform, but lowering his glance he saw that her legs, although slender, were unshapely, almost straight. 'Please,' he said, responding to Elizabeth Smith. He got out his notebook. If the woman's calmness was due to shock it may be that her story would differ later. Either way he had to record her eyewitness details.

'I had just dished up my supper and was about to sit down and eat it.' She glanced at the table in the window. There were no signs of a meal, eaten or otherwise. After telephoning the police she had scraped the haddock into the bin. 'I happened to notice a shadow on the wall. You see, the lighting here is such that if anyone walks up from the Bradley Road end, their shadow precedes them. Anyway, it was a man. A second or so later another man, wearing a football scarf, followed. It wasn't a Rickenham scarf. I noticed that because, well, to tell the truth, some of the fans scare me. I thought if the away team had been beaten and he was one of their supporters, he might be up to no good.'

Liz Blount returned with a tray of tea and set it on the table, pouring without interrupting.

'Almost immediately they'd passed the house I heard some scuffling then the sound of something metal being dropped. The next thing is the first man, the one without the scarf, was running back this way, towards Bradley Road.

'I went out there because it all seemed a bit odd.' She paused and inhaled deeply. 'Well, you know the rest. I rang the police and an ambulance.'

Markham nodded. It had been a reasonably lucid account. 'Mrs Smith, please don't take this personally, but were you sick?'

She looked down at her veined hands and blushed. 'Yes. I'm afraid I was. Does it matter?'

'No. Not at all. It's nothing to be ashamed of, it happens to police officers sometimes. But I had to ask. It'll save us taking a sample for evidence, to see if it was the victim's.' Not usually the most tactful of men, Markham wanted to keep on the right side of this witness. Her account rang true and if she was the type to watch habitually from her window she may have seen more than her mind was allowing her to recall. Still on his feet he strolled over to the window and stood about a foot away from the panes. The arc lights and part of the tent were visible without him leaning forward, nose against the glass, but it was unlikely that Mrs Smith would have seen the actual incident even if she had been standing in such a manner.

Twenty minutes later he had established that the two men were strangers to her, that even in the relative darkness of the street she could swear that she had never set eyes on either of them before. 'My long distance sight is good,' she said, 'but close to things are a bit of a blur without my glasses. I didn't have them on at the time, so I'm sure of what I'm telling you. The one who ran away,' she added thoughtfully, 'his footsteps echoed. So he couldn't have been wearing those awful trainer things. Oh, I'm sorry.'

'No offence taken,' Markham said, without looking down at his own feet. 'I might need to talk to you again, Mrs Smith. Thank you for your help.'

WPC Blount was polite enough to show him to the door and close it quietly behind him. Markham sighed with relief when he saw that the police tape across the end of the road was being removed to allow the pathologist's car through.

It was time to return to the station and put the 'murder room', as they called it, into action. Teams would be allocated various tasks. Further teams would follow them to double-check all the information gathered. It was going to be a long night. Saturday night too. Not that it mattered much to Markham, the murder had solved the problem of how he was to spend it.

If Mrs Smith was to be believed, she had related an odd sequence of events. Man A walks down the street. Man B, wearing a football scarf, follows. Man A turns around and attacks Man B then runs off back in the same direction from which he had come. Why not continue on through the park where there was less chance of being spotted? Unless Man A had wanted to be followed, had known, perhaps, that he was about to be attacked and acted first. Then where did the weapon come from? One or other of them had been armed in advance. Heavy spanners did not usually happen to be lying around in surburban streets.

And where the hell's Short? Markham wondered, as he made his way back to headquarters. But it wasn't his concern. For now he would continue to follow the procedure and let others worry about their new inspector.

Inspector Short sat at his desk digging around in his ear with a matchstick. He examined his findings beneath the harsh overhead lighting that also shone on his bald pate over which long strands of hair were carefully arranged. What he lacked on top was more than compensated for by the bedraggled moustache which concealed his top lip and the dark hairs which sprouted from the grubby cuffs of his shirt. With his stained tie, pudgy waistline and pallid complexion he looked deceptively unhealthy and resembled a seedy informer rather than a police officer. Hence his nickname Scruffy Short.

He had been made up to inspector ten years previously and was destined to remain at that rank, except for the occasional times he was acting up for someone. Not that he cared. He liked it where he was and claimed to be a truly contented man. This move now, he thought, is just another sideways one. There'd be no promotion for him here.

No one had ever been invited to his house but any invitation would probably have been refused. Short was not disliked, he was avuncular in his approach to colleagues and villains alike. It was simply that his colleagues feared his accommodation might match his appearance and therefore taking any form of refreshment there would be unthinkable.

Short had remained unmarried – understandably, in most people's opinion – although there were rumours that he had been seeing a woman for quite some time. That afternoon, on a legitimate break, Short had called in to see her. He had not heard his bleeper because at the time he and it and Nancy's plump limbs had been tangled in the bedclothes; and Nancy made a lot of noise.

Arriving back ten minutes late he had made contact with an officer at the scene and learned that Markham had taken charge. Short had deemed it not worth his while to turn up. Markham had cleared calling in the troops and the HQ pathologist with Superintendent Thorne. Short was aware that he might get a bollocking but it was better than getting cold. Besides, he and the Super knew where his talents lay and that was behind a desk. Of course he was supposed to attend a suspicious death but it was the scene-of-crime team who did the real work. What was the use of his being there when he was not allowed to touch anything? By no means a pen-pusher, he was too sharp for that, Short's skill was in being able to view the many facets of a case objectively from a distance. And it didn't seem to matter, not when there were men like Ian Roper who were only happy when they felt they 'knew' the victims and, for some peculiar reason, went out of their way to speak to all the suspects personally. Short preferred to meet them through their written statements, through indisputable evidence, then stand back and try to out-guess them.

'Ah, Markham.' Short didn't move a muscle when the door burst open and rebounded as the handle crashed against the wall.

'Where were you, sir?' The 'sir' was less than polite.

'On my break. I knew you'd handle it.'

'That isn't the point. You were supposed to be there.'

'You know me, Markham, I'd probably have only been in the way.' Short threw the matchstick into the bin.

Markham turned and left the room knowing that Short would follow. To a man who showered and shaved on a daily basis, the sight of Scruffy Short was repulsive.

An hour later as the house-to-house inquiries were taking place and the scene-of-crime officers were continuing their work in Alma Road, the men in the control room were already in possession of several facts concerning the victim. His name was Justin De Quincy, he was twenty-eight years old, he had not been mugged and it was likely that he was on his way home because he lived in Crossley Close on the opposite side of the small park at the end of Alma Road, in which direction he had been heading. All this information had come from his driving licence which was in his wallet, along with almost a hundred pounds in notes and seven different credit cards. His driving licence also contained penalty points for a motoring offence. That the wallet hadn't been planted on him for whatever nefarious reasons was about to be confirmed or otherwise. Two officers were on their way to the address given. They were hoping De Quincy had lived alone because then the task of informing relatives might fall to someone else. If there was a wife and children, well, they would do the best they could.

Meanwhile, Inspector Short, in his mild-mannered way, had assured Superintendent Thorne that the set-down procedure was being followed, that everything was up and running, but he omitted to mention his absence from Alma Road. He then sat back and mulled over the possibilities, infuriating Markham because he was able to suggest a logical viewpoint without having been there. 'It might be dead simple,' he said, tapping his teeth with a thumbnail before pulling at the ragged edges of his moustache. 'Local bloke, Ipswich supporter, say, sees the scarf. Few drinks inside him and thinks he'll show the bastard.' Uninterested in the game himself, he was aware from youthful experience in crowd control and from listening to men like Ian Roper and

Alan Campbell go on about it how deep feelings could run. DC Campbell supported a team called the Jags, whatever that might mean. The team played somewhere over the Scottish border and as far as Short was concerned it was the best place for them. However, he did have enough knowledge to recognise that Norwich was in Norfolk and Ipswich was in Suffolk and that therefore the two teams and their followers were local rivals. 'But if it's personal, then it's a different matter, although we stand more chance of finding him. Only one old dear rang in. What's the matter with them in Alma Road, are they all blind and deaf?'

'He was on foot.'

'What?' Short was fazed by Markham's non-sequitur.

'The assailant was on foot. Our only witness says he legged it back down the road the way he had come.'

'So what's to have stopped him parking in Bradley Road and following? There's no way out of Alma Road except by doing a three-point turn and giving everyone plenty of opportunity to clock your registration mark.'

'Exactly.'

'Exactly what?'

'He's local. If there was a car then he knew, as you said, that he couldn't risk driving down there. If he was on foot, then where did he come from? It's miles from the railway station, no buses service Bradley Road and you don't follow a pedestrian in a minicab.'

'Point taken. Okay, then, he's probably local. Only probably. Don't let's make too many assumptions too quickly. But the question still remains, was he lying in wait for De Quincy or did he just happen to see the scarf and decide to have a go?'

Markham shook his head. 'Why not wait until he reached the park? Why chance it there?'

'Drink. "For when the wine is in, the wit is out." Have you never woken up and wondered what the hell you were doing the night before?'

'Not often,' Markham replied with truth. And definitely not as often as you, he thought. He leaned back against a desk, hands in his pockets, still wearing his leather jacket despite the warmth of the building, and smiled malevolently. 'So how do you explain the weapon?'

Short had had enough of Markham and decided to be obtuse.

'He's a mechanic? He was going somewhere to help someone out? His heating system's broken down and he went to borrow a spanner from a mate?'

'You've just suggested he was drunk.'

'Went to borrow the spanner, stayed to have a few drinkies then things got out of hand. He sees the scarf, red rag to a bull, and gets all fired up. Does him in and drops the spanner – after all, it's not his – and flees. Later he'll tell his mate and everyone else how pissed he was and that he lost the said spanner on his way home. Someone else found it and used it for a purpose for which it was clearly not intended. Look, Markham, all this speculation is a total waste of time,' he concluded, leaving Markham speechless at the volte-face: it was Short who had started it. 'We need a witness who saw where he went. Why he was there is irrelevant. De Quincy's dead, our brief is to nick the man who killed him.'

The door opened and a through-draught ruffled the papers on the desk along with the loose strands combed across Short's scalp. No one in the room made eye contact for fear of laughing as the hair lifted and settled. From upstairs they had all, at one time or another, seen him cross the car-park below with the thin lock flying out at a right-angle above his left ear, his shiny pink scalp exposed.

At ten thirty Markham went home, surprised that Short had decided to remain until the first officers reported in with results from the house-to-house.

It was after midnight when Danny Cotton went home. He let himself into the darkened house quietly and locked up. From the landing a dim light showed. They left it on for the children in case they woke in the night. They were still young enough to tumble downstairs if they were half asleep.

'Jackie?' he whispered.

She did not answer, but in the faint wedge of light from the half-open bedroom door he saw her body stiffen beneath the bedclothes. Perhaps it's easier this way, he thought. If she's pretending to be asleep she won't ask any questions. Lately, they were both very good at pretending.

He went to the bathroom then checked on the children. The

older two were flushed with sleep and breathing evenly but the baby was snuffling. Danny pulled the blankets up over the plump little body in its white sleepsuit with the teddy bear pattern. He sighed. The children were beautiful and loved but how on earth would they cope with the fourth which was on the way? It was his fault. Jackie was unable to take the pill, he should have had the vasectomy as soon as they realised other methods did not work for them.

Danny returned to the bedroom and gazed at his wife as she breathed too evenly. Her short-cropped hair was dark, almost black against the white pillowcase. He loved her, he just couldn't get through to her lately. Naturally she was tired, but so was he.

'Jackie, I know you're awake. Please talk to me.'

She sat up in bed so suddenly that Danny jumped. 'About what? Look at the time. Do you want to talk about where you've been while I spent another night babysitting?'

'I don't know what's going wrong between us. I love you.'

He looks dreadful, Jackie thought. Perhaps he really has been doing overtime. Hadn't there been a murder? With two of the children demanding tea and the baby needing his last bottle she rarely took in the news fully. 'Get into bed before you freeze.'

Danny did so, grateful for the warmth of his wife's body. He took her hand in his and lay still for several minutes. Jackie, like himself, lay on her back staring at the ceiling.

'I really do love you,' he repeated, pulling her towards him. He stroked her stomach, already swollen, then slid his hand lower. It seemed impossible to be able to feel desire again so soon but he did and, better still, Jackie was responding.

'What's the matter?'

Danny flung himself over on his side, feeling close to tears. 'Nothing. I'm sorry. Too tired, that's all.' Jackie was already pregnant, there was no need to worry. It was guilt which rendered him impotent. And that, he thought, was the tragic irony. Because things had become so bad between them their sexual relationship had deteriorated and he had gone elsewhere. But because of this he could no longer perform at home.

'I'll be home early tomorrow,' he whispered. 'We'll talk then. We must get this sorted out.'

'Danny, if, as you say, you love me, then there's nothing to sort out, is there?' She spoke so coldly he felt frightened. Did she know? Had she guessed? If she had then it wouldn't be the whole truth. His mind was in a turmoil. Decisions had to be made but he did not think himself capable of making them.

He had heard the news and knew that a man was dead. Always short of money he had rung the station to see if there was any chance of overtime. He had not said anything then and now he never would. He was in the clear. No one had made the connection. And Emma was safe, too. It was she who had told him the man's name and his reason for being at Barbara Fletcher's house. But they didn't know about Barbara Fletcher either. Maybe now he could sleep a little easier at night.

3

Detective Constable Brenda Gibbons swivelled the rear-view mirror and checked her appearance. It was nine o'clock on Sunday morning and barely light. The car heater had warmed her up but the tip of her nose was still red. She wore little make-up and none in the summer. Her long, shimmering brown hair was naturally streaked with chestnut. She had tied it back in a scarf.

Shivering, she locked the car and walked towards the house in Crossley Close. Her boots and swagger coat were brown, her leather shoulder-bag matched. The only splash of colour was the orange and green scarf at her neck. But even in winter her clear skin and bright eyes radiated health.

Anne Morrisson appeared to be alone as she answered the door herself. She was fair and plump and probably pretty when she had not spent a whole sleepless night crying. She let Brenda in without speaking and took her along the thickly carpeted hall to the high-ceilinged room at the back of the house which even the miserable weather could not diminish. Brenda caught her breath. Whatever suffering had occurred during the night this house still had home etched into every part of it. The two settees were soft and plump and, like the armchairs, were covered in a warm apricot velvety material. Shades varying between cream and tan merged into one another and the walnut furniture was highly polished. On several small tables were lamps, unlit now, and a vase of chrysanthemums whose autumnal scent filled the warm room. Through the patio doors Brenda saw a well-tended garden although there were few flowers now. Those in the vase had, she realised, been cut from the late stragglers in one of the borders. One day I shall own somewhere like this, she thought in the few seconds' space before she got down to business.

'They offered to find someone to stay with me but I wanted to be on my own,' Anne said, as if an explanation was required. Her voice was low and soft. 'I said that my sister was coming, it's true, she is, but I wanted last night to myself.'

'I understand. Some people prefer it that way. Can I get you something? Tea or coffee, or something to eat?'

Anne Morrisson shook her head and sat down heavily. Brenda followed suit, choosing the settee opposite the one where Anne sat in order to be able to face her. The young woman was too distressed to be bothered with social niceties and would have left her standing.

'I need to ask you some questions. I can come back later if you'd prefer?'

There was a slight hesitation. Anne squeezed her forehead between thumb and fingers as she decided whether putting it off would be cowardly. 'No. You might as well stay.'

No rings, Brenda noted. 'How long have you known Justin?'

'Five years. We've lived together for the last three. Here. In this house. We're buying it jointly.'

Were buying it jointly, Brenda corrected silently. She hoped Anne would receive De Quincy's share, it would be one less burden for her to shoulder. This woman had loved her man and was genuinely grieving. Brenda had lost her husband, Harry, to other women and had finally lost him altogether when his violence became intolerable and she had thrown him out. How different were their lots. 'Did he work here, in Rickenham Green?'

'Oh, no. In London. He's got a flat there. He only comes home at weekends.'

Complications already, Brenda thought. Two circles of people with whom he was involved. She continued to use the past tense even though Anne was unable to do so.

'He's in the City. What they call a trader.' She spoke with a touch of pride. 'He's doing really well. That's why he can afford

31

two places. I didn't want to live in London. If I had . . .' Her face sagged as the sentence trailed off.

'Did he often go to football matches?'

Ann stopped chewing a nail and looked up, frowning. 'No. He's taken important people to Wembley, the Cup Final, things like that, but he's not particularly into football.'

'I see. Anne, where was he yesterday afternoon?'

'He'd arranged to play squash with a friend. They usually have a couple of drinks afterwards, that's why he didn't have the car.' She shook her head as more tears welled up.

Brenda waited. Life was so full of ifs. Had he driven, would De Quincy still be alive? But perhaps he had lied to her, perhaps he thought it was unfair on Anne to go and watch a match when he hadn't seen her all week but he knew her well enough to realise she would accept him playing squash after being cooped up in an office. No. No logic there. He could have played squash every night of the week in London and Anne would have known that. 'Do you know this friend's name?'

'Yes. It was a regular fortnightly arrangement. Justin didn't think it was fair to me to play every week. Andrew Osborne. He lives out at Frampton. Pardon?'

Brenda had spoken at the same time, echoing the word Frampton. What a bloody small world, she thought cynically. Now she, or someone, would have to interview the man whom she had been seeing over the past few months; a personal injury solicitor with a tall, ungainly body and a pock-marked face who had also been through a disastrous marriage. Neither she nor Andrew had children and they were in agreement that they were not ready to make any sort of commitment. She wondered just how close she and Andrew were. She was aware that Andrew played squash but until last night she had never heard of Justin De Quincy. 'Were they good friends?'

'Oh, no, I never met him. Andrew, that is. Justin said Andrew had once been looking for a partner and the time suited them both and they had continued from there. But they didn't see each other outside the club.'

Thank goodness, Brenda thought. De Quincy might have been murdered because he was on the wrong side of the law and it would not look good for Andrew, especially in his profession, if he was found to have been fraternising with a criminal. 'Anne, did Justin own a football scarf?'

'No. The only scarf he's got is his university one and he keeps that for sentimental reasons, he doesn't wear it.'

'What time were you expecting him back?'

'About six thirty, seven, he was never later than that. I was just beginning to worry. I'd prepared . . .' but she couldn't go on.

Brenda pictured her spending the afternoon in the kitchen making a special meal.

The last question had to be asked although she could guess the answer. No one who loses a person they love through murder can believe someone would wish them harm.

'No. No, absolutely not.' Anne was adamant he had no enemies.

'Someone perhaps you didn't know, someone he may have given bad financial advice to?'

She shook her head violently. It was the first spark of life she had shown. 'He said he was going places, that the one thing he'd never do is discuss his work, he'd seen others get into trouble. In fact, I don't think anyone here even knows what he does. He used to say he had a boring office job which happened to pay well.' The small smile was that of a proud mother. 'That isn't true, of course. He loves his work, the excitement, the highs. He really needed his weekends here to unwind.'

Brenda noticed the use of the mixed tenses, the gradual acceptance of what could not be altered. 'Look, when you feel up to it, would you be prepared to make a list of everyone he knew? Everyone you can think of with whom he came into contact?'

'I can try. I'm not sure about the London side, although I've heard a few names.'

'Thank you. We'll be in touch. This is my card. Please feel free to ring me at any time, even if it's only for a chat. Will you be all right?'

Anne assured her that she would be, that her sister was due to arrive about midday.

Brenda decided to leave it at that.

Driving back to the station she wondered about a man who lived by taking risks, who, in fact, seemed to thrive on it. Just how far would such a man go? And in what direction?

She reported in to the control room then went to the open-plan general office where detectives worked from desks each fitted with its own computer terminal and two telephones. About to ring Andrew she saw he had beaten her to it. There was a message asking her to contact him as soon as possible. De Quincy's relatives had all been informed of his death and his name had been released to the media that morning. Andrew would have heard it on the news and realised that someone would want to question him. With a deep sigh she lifted the receiver to tell him that someone other than herself would need to speak to him.

'Hello?' Moira's voice was light and cheerful as she picked up the phone on Sunday afternoon because she expected it to be Mark. Ian was in the bathroom with the radio playing on the landing. He was listening to a concerto on Radio 3. 'Yes, he is. Hold on, please.'

'Ian, it's for you,' she called up the stairs, coughing slightly because of the smell of paint which had permeated the house since Tuesday. Ian's new hobby was certainly keeping him occupied. He had begun on the bathroom first thing that morning.

They had had a really nice evening at the Duke of Clarence and had returned home for a nightcap and chatted until the small hours. That morning Ian had got out the paintbrush as soon as he'd eaten a piece of toast but had stopped to take a brisk walk with Moira which had ended at the Crown where they had eaten beef sandwiches with their drinks. Immediately upon their return he had gone back to the decorating. He still had another few days' leave and was talking about doing a third room.

'Pardon?'

'The telephone. Didn't you hear it?'

Moira stood beside him as he took the call. His expression was a mixture of grimness and disappointment.

'Oh, no, Ian,' Moira said, guessing at the contents of the conversation. 'Can't they cope without you even for a few days?'

'Sorry, love. My going in isn't compulsory. Oh, God, I really don't want to.'

She saw that he meant it, that this was no platitude to placate her. For the first time she could recall he had been thoroughly

34

enjoying himself in his free time. She was more disappointed for him than for herself. After all, she'd be at work in the morning.

Ian followed her to the kitchen. It had been a lovely weekend. As despondent as Moira that their enjoyment had been spoiled and his new love, decorating, interrupted, he said quietly, 'There's been another murder.'

'What?' She turned to face him, her blue eyes wide with surprise. 'Two? In less than twenty-four hours?'

Ian's own eyes, a greyish-green, softened. He saw that Moira understood, that she knew he would find it impossible to relax knowing that he was needed. And there was something else, another reason for not wishing to go back yet. 'Oh, hell.'

'What is it?'

'Scruffy Short. I've been trying to forget he was joining us. He was due to start on Monday.'

'Is he the one who's taken Barry's place?'

'Sort of. I think he just gets shifted around every time a team gets fed up with him. Will you be all right?'

Moira smiled. 'Ian, how many times have I been left on my own?' It was not an unkind remark, she was simply reassuring him that he need not worry about her. And if he really could fit in his next leave to coincide with hers it might, in the end, be worth this interruption because, with the days he was about to forfeit, they would be able to have a longer break together.

He picked up his winter coat and his car keys from the hall table, kissed the top of Moira's head and left the house.

The car refused to start until the fourth attempt. Ian cursed. Once the engine was running he scraped the ice from the windows and sat in the driver's seat. Did he really want this? Hadn't he taken his leave because he was exhausted? And he had been revelling in the decorating. It was hard to imagine he had scoffed at people who boasted about their DIY efforts. But to stay at home when help was needed? No, that was unthinkable. With a sigh he manoeuvred the car out from between two others and headed towards the town centre.

It was already dark and there was no one in the streets, not even the homeless of which Rickenham, like everywhere else, had acquired its share. Ian wondered how they could possibly survive in these bleak conditions. The answer was that some didn't. A dog trotted along the pavement, tail held high. It stopped to sniff at a tree trunk then cocked its leg. One or two cars were on the roads but little else moved. The world seemed almost at a standstill; its inhabitants might have been hibernating.

He drove down the deserted High Street. The cinema was lit but there was no one in the foyer as all three performances were under way. The take-away outlets which now seemed to dominate the town were bright and welcoming, but empty. He turned left to where the unsightly office blocks and the new Town Hall stood. The youngish trees in their brick surrounds were more than saplings now but still looked frail. White lights behind unbreakable plastic glowed along the walls of the police station car-park and made the frost on the cars sparkle. The roses in the raised beds had been pruned almost to the ground. Their vicious thorny remains pointed blackly to the sky.

It felt as though he had been away for a month when he pushed his way through the swing doors and the familiar odour filled his nostrils. It surprised him that nothing had changed. With a wave to the man on the front desk he mounted the stairs and went straight to the control room. Only three people were present. DC Alan Campbell was reading something with a concentrated frown, DC Brenda Gibbons was sitting on a chair, legs crossed, one swinging lethargically, and the dreaded Inspector Short was staring out of the window, his hands in his pockets. Ian was furious. He had been dragged away from home where he'd been having a good time because of a so-called panic and a shortage of staff and those that were on duty appeared to be doing nothing. And now he would have to try to be pleasant to Short.

'Sir.' Brenda saw him first and stood up although the formality was not necessary.

'Ah, good to see you, Chief.' Short's smile was genuinely welcoming.

God, Ian thought, I must've been a wicked man in some previous life to deserve this. He had known Short was coming but had tried to pretend it wasn't really going to happen. The man was a slob, no doubt about that, and although Moira nagged Ian about his appearance, it was more for his habit of hanging on to clothes for far too long rather than for the total scruffiness that Short possessed. And the man was unreliable. No, that was

36

unfair. Unpunctual at times and often where he shouldn't be, but nevertheless a good man. If only he wasn't so damn jovial all the time, Ian thought, realising that this was the core of the matter. No matter how much shit was thrown at him Short still had the ability to smile whereas Ian's moods were apparent to everyone because he was incapable of disguising them. 'Brenda?' He had noticed the small furrow of her brow as she frowned.

'It's Andrew.' Don't say it, she begged silently, don't dare call him the ugly brute.

'Is he ill?'

'No. He knew De Quincy. We've got his statement already, he volunteered it. Alan took it,' she added quickly.

'And?' Ian knew as much or as little as the general public did about the first murder. After Moira's Saturday evening panic over his own well-being, they had listened to news bulletins over the course of the weekend. Ian was aware of the deceased's name but little more than that so far.

'Andrew confirms what the girlfriend said.'

'Hang on. Fill me in first.' Brenda did so. 'And Andrew's part in all this?'

'Both he and Anne Morrisson say they met on a two-weekly basis at the club. They played squash for an hour, showered, had one or two drinks then each went their separate ways. It was no different yesterday. Andrew says he knew very little about the man other than that he worked in London and came home at the weekends because he had a girlfriend here.'

'Then you can stop worrying about him. He's in the clear. When did De Quincy leave the squash club?'

'Quarter-past six, give or take a minute or two. Half a dozen members have verified it. None of them claim to know him well either. He only put in an appearance on his fortnightly visits and never attended social functions.'

'So there was no time unaccounted for, not if they found him in Alma Road just after six thirty.' Not one to walk if it could be avoided, even Ian realised De Quincy had not had the chance to go elsewhere, nor could he have stopped for a long chat. Unless he was given a lift part of the way. 'London life?'

'The Met's checking for us.'

'Good. Second victim?' Ian addressed the question to Short.

'David Walters. White male. Age forty-one. Married. One daughter. He worked as a hospital porter. He was stabbed as he came off duty.'

'Not St Luke's in Alma Road?' For a second Ian imagined that the killer had struck twice in almost the same place.

'No. Rickenham General.'

There was a psychiatric unit attached which prompted Ian to ask, 'Were all the patients accounted for?'

'Yep. The new wing houses neurotics mostly. More serious cases still go to Mounthaven or St Martin's.' Short chewed at the straggling hair on his upper lip. 'By all accounts the wife's hysterical. We can't get any sense out of her because all she can say is, "I knew it. I knew this would happen." Her GP's sedated her. The daughter's about twelve. Different temperament altogether. Visibly shocked but quite calm. Nothing much could be done without her mother present but I reckon the girl'll make more sense in the end.'

'You were there? At the Walters' place?' Ian was surprised.

'No. I've been told.'

'What time was the body discovered?'

'Four thirty. Nurse returning to duty from her tea break. She'd been back to her room for something.'

'And Walters finished at what time?'

'Three thirty.'

Ian nodded. It could mean that the nurse had discovered him immediately after he was killed, in which case he had been elsewhere in the hospital during that period. Visiting a nurse in her room? Had he angered a jealous boyfriend? Walters was around the right age to have become tempted. Marrried, what? fifteen, maybe twenty years, a daughter about to enter her teens, the onset of the male menopause? Not that he was sure if such a thing existed, it was more than likely another modern, meaningless phrase which had crept into common parlance. However, he thought, even if he was killed immediately after coming off duty they did not need a pathologist to estimate the time of death, there was only one hour during which it could have happened. Perhaps that was what the wife had meant when she said she had known it would happen. Maybe he *had* been a naughty boy and she had warned him it would end in tears.

'Not a pretty sight, our man Walters. The knife had made several entry points. Someone wanted to make certain.'

Ian raised an eyebrow and Brenda smiled in response. Yes, Short had put in an appearance at the scene.

There was silence for several seconds. Ian sighed and ran a hand through his thick, springy hair. It was noticeably greying above his ears now and it depressed him each time he looked in a mirror. He consoled himself with the thought that if, as an old man, he began to lose inches as his father had done, he would still be tall. Even four inches off his height would leave him standing at six feet and, thanks to Moira's constant vigilance, his waistline was under control. Mostly. Returning to work had depressed him. Ian became aware that the silence was continuing. He glanced around the room.

'It's odd, sir, the scarves.'

Three pairs of eyes turned to Alan Campbell who had, until that moment, remained silent. It was typical that he was off at a tangent yet what he said came from a direct line of thought. His Scottish accent had mellowed but remained unmistakable. Had he lost it altogether his looks would still have declared his origins. Sandy hair topped an almost alabaster complexion which was sprinkled with gingery freckles. His seemingly lashless eyes were a faded blue and he looked undernourished which was impossible because Alan Campbell ate continuously. 'I was trying to work out a connection, you see.' He had blushed, as he frequently did when putting forward an opinion or a theory. 'Why would someone like De Quincy who wasn't interested in the game wear a Norwich City scarf?' The word 'game' only ever meant football to Alan. 'Walters, on the other hand, did go to matches, but apparently only watched Rickenham Athletic, and then only infrequently.'

'You mean both men wore a Canaries scarf?' Ian was incredulous. Football? Was there a correlation between the two cases? 'Perhaps De Quincy borrowed his from someone at the squash club. It was a bitterly cold day,' he suggested. 'Are you sure both scarves were the same and not just the same combination of colours?'

'Yes. And I've already checked,' Brenda said. 'Neither man owned such a scarf, at least according to their women.'

39

'You didn't say,' Alan retorted accusingly. A precise man, a lover of cross-referencing and double-checking, he felt he had been made to appear uninformed.

Brenda bit her lip. 'It's my fault, sir,' she admitted. 'I only found out half an hour ago, and, well, I forgot . . .' The sentence trailed off but Ian did not require any further explanation. Everyone in the room was aware how anxious Brenda had been about Andrew Osborne's involvement.

'Okay. But don't let it happen again. Small details are important, as we all know. Where were we? Let's get into their backgrounds. Two murders in almost as many days. It's not unheard of but hardly par for the course here. So, yes, let's try for a connection.' But even as he spoke Ian thought this was unlikely. A hospital porter with a family, and a trader in the City; a thirteen-year difference in their ages which would lessen the likelihood of their knowing each other socially, one beaten to death, the other stabbed.

Until late that night they sifted through the sparse information to hand. Soon there would be mounds of it, most of it useless, but somewhere there would be something, no matter how insignificant, which would hold the key.

On the negative side there was only one witness in the Alma Road killing, although Elizabeth Smith had not actually seen it taking place, and there had been none in the hospital grounds. It had now been established that David Walters had left at his usual time, immediately his shift had finished. Ian's head jerked up. 'Have you seen this?' He shoved a hastily and badly typed report across the desk.

Brenda read aloud what the officer who had questioned the hospital staff had written. 'Walters had been employed as a porter for less than a year. He carried out his duties efficiently and without question but other porters on his shift along with the theatre sister and ward sisters with whom he worked all claim they knew nothing about his personal life and that he rarely spoke to anyone unless it was necessary.'

Brenda nodded in recognition of this vague connection, as did Short. Alan Campbell chewed his lip. Just because the two victims were taciturn did not actually mean anything. Not unless they both had something to hide.

'If only it were that simple,' Ian said, getting up wearily. 'I'm going home.'

Markham looked at his watch. There was an hour and a half before the pubs closed. If he glanced through the social worker's report on Richard Andrews there would be just enough time for a last drink in the Black Horse. It was still on his desk, as yet unopened because of the intervening events.

'Verbose, or what?' he asked himself half-way through. He could have written it using a quarter of the words. He made notes as he wrote; they formed a précis of the whole.

Born to affluent parents. Mother much younger than father. Mother left when Richard was seven. Unhappy childhood because of indifference of parents. Father's indifference increased when mother left. Sent to public school where befriended by Martin Cooper. Strong bond formed, lasting to adulthood.

Markham paused. Cooper had been his only friend. No wonder it had hit him so hard when he died. He pictured the huddled figure at the graveside on that bitter January morning. Markham had watched from a distance. There were few mourners. It had been a sad reflection on the life of such a vital young man. Martin's parents had flown back from abroad; apart from them there was only an aunt and Richie Andrews whose head had remained bowed the whole time Markham had observed him. The leafless trees had an armour of ice and seemed to stand at attention as the pallbearers carried the coffin to the gaping hole. Markham had followed at a distance, the frosted grass crunching beneath his feet. Richie had been the only one to pick up a handful of the crystallised earth which had glittered in the winter sun. Tears had run down his face as he crumbled the soil between his fingers and scattered it over the lowered coffin. Even then Markham had felt an affinity with the boy, perhaps because he, too, felt alone.

He was shocked by this unusual introspection and fanciful imagery of the cemetery. Almost human, he thought, and grinned, causing a passing detective to walk on more quickly. There always seemed to be more malevolence than humour in Markham's smiles.

41

He read on, continuing to make notes. Richard Andrews spent more and more time at the Coopers' house, usually in the care of staff as senior Coopers mostly absent. High achievers, both boys. Cooper gained place at Cambridge, Andrews was to follow one year later. When Cooper was sent down, Andrews forfeited his own place.

The youths had been that close. Markham had not realised it at the time. They had ended up in London in a flat Cooper's parents bought for him. Washed their hands of him, I suppose, Markham thought, but too proud to have the lad on the dole. Andrews' father, likewise. He had continued to pay him an allowance.

So why Rickenham? What was in it here for them? And why has Andrews stayed? One crime, one recorded crime and Cooper ends up dead. Markham flipped to the police notes. They had been seen breaking and entering and were caught on the job. What was it Cooper had shouted as he and Johnny Vaughan flung themselves into the van? 'He isn't involved' – something like that. And Andrews had been left behind as they sped off, a police car in pursuit. On their way to London Cooper had lost control of the vehicle and hit the concrete stanchion of a bridge. Both boys were killed instantly. Leaving Richie Andrews alone again, Markham concluded. How would he feel in the same situation? He had been in it once but had made a point of never getting close enough to anyone to allow it to happen again and therefore could not answer his own question. Life was far simpler if lived in isolation. Except for the job. That, he suspected, kept him sane. Smiling again as he locked up the files, he knew that other people might not agree with him.

Curiosity led him past Richie Andrews' flat on his way to the Black Horse. A light was on but the curtains were closed. Markham shook his head. He had no reason whatsoever to speak to him. But he knew that he wanted to.

Ten thirty; Sunday drinking hours were a pain. But Markham had managed to drink three pints of lager in forty-five minutes. Normally he paced himself but for some reason he felt in need of the buzz they produced. Enough, but not enough to make him drunk. He forgot about Andrews as he watched the other customers taking their time over their drinks. He knew perfectly well that the landlord served after hours, and the landlord knew he knew, but he could not afford to do so blatantly. He was waiting for Markham to leave.

'Time,' he called. 'Hurry up with your glasses, please. You'd think some of them lived here the way they carry on,' he said, addressing Markham.

Markham swallowed the last of his drink and turned to leave. 'Some of them virtually do,' he said with a wink.

Inspector Short surprised his colleagues two nights in a row. He was also the last to leave on Sunday. He was there when the report came in of a suspicious-looking man loitering in a small park which happened to be not far from where Ian lived. Normally a team in a patrol car would have been sent to investigate and dealt with the matter and that would have been the end of it. But because of the two murders CID had requested that they were informed of all suspicious incidents.

Short read the message. 'He's big,' the complainant had said. 'He's been standing there for ages, I can see him from my window because of the streetlights. He's waving his arms around and shouting. It's upsetting my wife. I wonder if someone could do something about him?'

But when a patrol car turned up the man had gone.

A nutter? Short wondered. It's always possible. He tried to picture a man deranged enough to pick on random victims and kill them but he couldn't. Instead he focused his thoughts on Nancy. Was it too late to pop round? She can always say no, he thought as he reached for his coat.

4

On Monday morning, during the briefing which covered both murders, the team were allotted their duties.

Brenda nodded glumly when she and Alan Campbell were given the far from pleasant task of calling on Anne Morrisson and asking her if she was aware of the existence of the woman with whom De Quincy had shared his London flat during the week. They knew Anne worked full time in an estate agent's office and that on the rare occasions they spent the weekend in London the other girl, Charlotte Jones, would be safely in Devon visiting her parents. But of course *she* didn't know. De Quincy had gone to an awful lot of trouble to prevent her finding out.

Brenda had pondered over the question of how he managed to hide the evidence of his other life, even temporarily, until she learned how it had been achieved. Clothes, toiletries, make-up and personal possessions would all have needed to be hidden. Even the odd stray hair might have aroused suspicion. No wonder the Met had been slow in getting back to them. The address Anne had given them was that of a bachelor called Jeremy Fisher. He had been questioned discreetly at first but it had taken the news of his friend's death before he came out with the truth.

'I used to lend him this place so's he could bring his girlfriend here. His other girlfriend. The one he lives with, Charlotte, owns her own place. He stays there during the week. I'm mostly away at weekends, so it was no skin off my nose and it meant the place wasn't left empty,' Jeremy had finally confessed. 'Anne believed he lived here.'

But there were still things which puzzled Brenda – for instance, what happened if she wanted to ring him? Justin could not have given her Charlotte's number in case Charlotte answered the phone or wanted to know who he was talking to. A mobile phone, I suppose, she concluded. 'Come on,' she said to Alan with resignation. 'Let's get it over with.' Anne had enough to cope with without whatever this news would do to her. Brenda imagined it would be like a double death. But there had been some rapport between the two women so she realised she had to be the one to go.

Alan threw his plastic coffee container into the bin with perfect aim. He screwed up the wrapper from the Kit-Kat he had just eaten and that followed it, then he opened the door for Brenda and they left the building, stepping out into the cold winter's morning made more gloomy by the dull, grey sky.

Her lot's not that much different from mine after all, Brenda realised as she backed the car out of its parking space. She was driving because Alan had taken an apple from his pocket and

44

had begun munching it on his way to the car. Anne Morrisson had believed herself happy until she had lost her man. Brenda had known fairly quickly what an awful mistake it was to have married Harry. She, too, had lost her man, but in her case it was a relief. Anne now had to bear her grief and the knowledge of his infidelity at the same time.

The ice on the windscreen melted fast once she started the engine and the remaining slivers slipped off the side windows as she drove off. The sky was so low it appeared to rest on the tops of the buildings. The faces of pedestrians were pinched and many were red-nosed. Sudden gusts of icy wind swept inland from the English Channel, flinging litter across the car bonnet and taking people by surprise as their clothes ballooned around them. Brenda hated the winter although the colouring of the seasonal clothes suited her, bringing out the russet in her hair and the brownness of her eyes with their hazel glints. She was dressed in an olive skirt, cream blouse and a buttonless thigh-length cardigan in a slightly paler shade of green. Over this, even in the car, she had on her tan wool coat. It seemed hard to remember that only four months ago she had lain on the sand at Southwold and sweltered.

They were almost there. She glanced across at Alan who had been about to shove the apple core into the glove compartment before catching her eye and deciding to get rid of it elsewhere. 'I don't want to do this,' Brenda said.

'Me, neither, but it'll be better coming from you.'

She did not bother to ask what he meant. However hard he tried, Alan could not overcome his inherited prejudices. Women might be the weaker sex, but this was definitely woman's work. She pulled up outside Anne Morrisson's house, took a deep breath and got out of the car.

B team were now following up on the house-to-house inquiries which their predecessors had initiated regarding Justin De Quincy's death. And there were still some people in Alma Road who had not been questioned because they had been away for the weekend. Naturally they would have seen nothing but they might have noticed something prior to the event. Those who had been seen might remember some small detail which had

45

previously eluded them. These officers were aware that their reception would not always be good. A certain type of person would not want to be bothered again and would tell them so. Other officers were despatched to the hospital, the squash club and the homes of the neighbours of David Walters. Two murders at once was more than a strain on their manpower. Ian was still waiting to receive lists of all the friends, relatives, business contacts and work colleagues of the two men. It might be a long wait. Anne Morrisson was about to receive another shock and if Pat Walters was still in the same state as when she initially received the news she would be unable to provide any information. The City of London police, along with the Met, were investigating De Quincy's working and social life there and had had the unpleasant task of breaking the news to Charlotte Jones. Later Ian might pay her a visit himself. She, too, was in the same position as Anne Morrisson, having to learn of the existence of another woman in De Quincy's life.

Markham, left more or less to his own devices, would be where he worked best: out on the streets 'having a word' with his informers and passing the time of day with known violent offenders who happened not to be in jail.

It was down to Ian to visit the widow Walters and her daughter. She had claimed to know Walters' death was inevitable. He certainly wanted to find out why. But with two females in the house, possibly three if Patricia Walters had a friend comforting her, he would need one of his own to be present throughout the interview.

He took one last glance at the map on the wall where a couple of drawing pins with coloured heads were all there was to show where two deaths had taken place. The pictures pinned up beside it told a different story. Ian had to rely on a uniformed WPC to accompany him. He decided to ask if Liz Blount was available. She had been partially involved in the first murder; there was always the chance that she might notice some similarity. He was lucky: she was on duty but not involved in anything which took priority over his request.

Once his lungs had recovered from the shock of the first inhalation of icy air, Ian breathed deeply and led Liz Blount towards the pool car which would take them to their destination. Their breath streamed from the corners of their mouths in the strengthening wind which indicated that the temperature was rising, even if they couldn't feel the difference.

The scarves were still puzzling Ian, as they were everyone else. If the men hadn't owned them, where had they come from and why had they been draped around the necks of the bodies? Was it simply down to a football grievance? Or was someone, knowing where Ian's allegiance lay, having a laugh by trying to confuse him?

Forget it, he thought, as he bent his tall frame almost in half in order to climb into the back seat of the car. The driver already had the engine running. He engaged first gear and pulled away as Ian settled into a more comfortable position. As he did so he caught a glimpse of his face in the rear-view mirror. His expression was stern and there seemed to be more than the usual amount of lines fanning out from around his eyes.

I bloody well shouldn't be here, he told himself as he was conveyed towards the home of the second murder victim. I'm supposed to be on leave. I could've finished the bathroom and started on our bedroom by now. He was pleased to discover that WPC Blount was just as content as himself to endure the journey in silence.

David Walters' house was much as Ian had imagined it to be from the address given. At a time when Rickenham Green had been rapidly expanding, the council had seen fit to name the necessary new public highways after Suffolk rivers. As they were not that numerous it had led to some rethinking and not a little confusion. For instance, because of the lack of choice, there was Deben Road, Deben Lane and Deben Avenue and, apart from the people who lived there, few were able to give accurate directions if asked. However, before that time, when the town had not yet outgrown its Victorian persona despite a world war having taken place, the houses being built were large and detached with enough room for live-in staff whom, until the outbreak of the next war, most people retained. These near-mansions lined wide streets. But Street was not a word to attract prospective residents so the paved and tarmacked thoroughfares were called Grove or Orchard or Copse, preceded by some equally pastoral name such as Linden or Beech or Maple.

But there was yet another distinction. If the name of a tree was followed by Road this would mean an area of three-bedroomed semis with garages and just enough land to be called a garden. It was to one of these that Ian was heading.

Ian hated change and, given his own way, would have left Rickenham Green as it had been two hundred years ago: the pub and a smattering of cottages which surrounded three sides of the actual green after which the then hamlet had been named. These properties were now in the hands of conservationists and sold for large amounts of money. St Luke's church with its pretty lych-gate and churchyard had become half hidden by the monstrosity of a supermarket and its car-park. Behind it, on one of the few gentle hills which existed in the county, where sheep and cows had once grazed, tiers of council houses had been built. Ever bloody outwards, he thought belligerently, picturing the outskirts of the town with their superstores and roundabouts and the eyesore of Rickenham General Hospital built inconveniently out of people's reach. Which thought brought him back to the matter at hand and what he would find at 21 Aspen Road where Patricia Walters was expecting him.

Walking up the short path, Liz Blount trying to keep up with his lengthy stride, he recalled Moira's recent accusation that he was turning into a sour old man. He knew that his idealism was misplaced, that originally the cottages on the green had been no more than hovels and that those who dwelled within them were poor and disease-ridden. And brides still stood, smiling, in the lych-gate of St Luke's, full of optimism, so many of them to be disappointed. Without growth there would be more unemployment and certainly no job for himself.

The lower half of all the houses was of red brick, the upper white-painted pebble-dash. They had plain, oblong windows with metal frames, steeply sloping roofs and an abundance of neatness. Not one black bin liner marred the street.

The door opened before he could knock and Ian had to adjust his sights. He had been expecting a woman to answer, but it was the daughter who had been watching out for him.

'Are you Inspector Roper?' she asked.

He did not bother to correct her as to his rank but produced his identity and showed it to her, because he was certain that she had been about to ask to see it.

The girl, Debbie, nodded. 'Mum's in here.'

He was shown into the front room where he needed to adjust his eyes for a second time. Any light from the dull day was further blocked out by the nets at the window and heavy drapes a quarter drawn on each side, but it was otherwise a comfortable family room. Open bookshelves filled with well-thumbed books lined one wall. A sewing basket stood open, revealing numerous reels of coloured cotton. On the brown cord sofa was a bundle of knitting. Even to Ian's inexpert eye the garment was too large to have been destined for either Pat Walters or her daughter. It was the trivia of married life, but far from trivial. That unfinished jumper would be a constant reminder to Pat Walters.

'She's got a headache,' Debbie said. 'I expect it's what the doctor gave her.'

As she quietly left the room Ian was surprised at her maturity.

'Would you like some tea?' Pat Walters spoke from an arm-chair. She was diminutive with short dark hair. They must have made quite a contrast. David had been meaty and blond. Her voice was just above a whisper.

'Only if you're having some.'

'Yes. I think I will. Please sit down, both of you.' She got up and left the room, moving gracefully despite her grief.

WPC Blount knew her job. She was there as a precaution or perhaps to put an arm around a shoulder if necessary. She had no qualms about equality, there were few men who knew how to comfort a woman. She took the corner of the sofa which placed her at right angles to where Pat had been sitting, leaving the armchair opposite for the chief inspector.

Ian quickly assimilated the internal neatness which matched his first impressions from the outside. The fact that the decent furniture was now shabby did nothing to lessen the homely feel of the place. Not usually susceptible to atmosphere and despite the present grief it contained, Ian sensed he was in a house which had sheltered a real family who loved each other. Doing the best they could on not much money, he summarised.

Pat returned as silently as she had left the room, closing the door behind her. It was warm, but not unpleasantly so, the radiators set at a sensible temperature. Ian took off his sheepskin jacket and laid it across the back of his chair. 'Debbie's making the tea. She's been absolutely wonderful. I don't think I could've coped without her.' Tears filled her eyes but she held them in check with a small sniff as she sat down again, folding her legs beneath her and her arms across her chest as if protecting herself.

Ian assumed she was referring to the events of the weekend. His subconscious produced a mental image of Mark, his and Moira's only child. A man now, an artist who, to Ian's surprise, was earning a living from his painting in Italy. It seemed only yesterday Ian had tried to teach him to kick a football only to discover his son had no interest in any sport other than tennis. Mark had always been closer to Moira. If Ian were killed their son would be to his mother what Debbie was to Pat Walters. If anything happened to Moira he and Mark would grieve separately, Ian thought, heavy with sadness. He wondered if he was going down with something. He was not usually so introspective when on a big case. And then he noticed a small peeling corner of wallpaper near the ceiling and, to his utter horror, felt a strong urge to stick it back in place. What's happening to me? he thought as he forced himself to listen.

'When they told me, well, I thought, I imagined, but I couldn't believe he'd use a knife. He was the most non-violent man I've ever met. That was the trouble, I suppose.'

Ian studied her chalk white face and the dead look in her eyes and wondered if her GP had miscalculated the strength of the tranquilliser. The smaller the person, the less the dosage, even he knew that much. Pat Walters appeared almost anorectic and she had not got that way overnight. And she seemed to be talking incoherently.

'Who? Who wouldn't use a knife?' Ian asked quietly, wondering if she had guessed the killer's identity.

'Dad, of course.' It was Debbie who spoke. She had inherited her mother's ability to move around without being heard. She stood in the doorway with a tray in her hands. 'I'll be in my room if you need me, Mum,' she said, having placed the tray on the coffee table.

'Thanks, love. I'll be fine.'

'David? Your husband?'

Pat was about to get up. Liz Blount raised a hand and said she would see to the tea.

'Dave. I always called him Dave. You can't imagine what it's been like. Living with the fear. I'd been expecting it for the past year.' She laughed, albeit mirthlessly, but Ian and Liz were both shocked. 'He was late home from work. That was nothing new. He needed time to himself, I understood that. In every other way he was a perfect husband. Just an hour here and there, he never neglected us. That's why I wasn't any more worried than usual. And the hospital buses aren't always reliable on a Sunday. Then, when the police knocked on the door, I knew he was dead.

'It was only a matter of time, you see. You'd have had to have known him to understand. He was kind and gentle and loving and that was his downfall. Perhaps all new widows speak highly of their husbands, but in this case it's true.'

Although Ian was not sure what she was getting at, Pat Walters now spoke with complete clarity and with such quiet determination that he knew what he was hearing was not drug-induced but the truth.

'You may check his background as much as you like. You won't find anything, not even another woman. I'm not a fool, chief inspector. I knew my man,' she added, making eye contact for the first time. 'Other people, given time, would have got over it. Not Dave, he could never forgive himself. That day changed him for ever.' She had said her piece. With reasonably steady hands she reached forwards for her tea. 'And that,' she concluded tearfully, 'is the bloody irony of it.'

Ian experienced momentary anger. What day? Was there something he hadn't been told? Had DC Brenda Gibbons, mooning about over the ugly brute, forgotten to pass on vital information? If so, short-staffed or not, she was off the case. But Pat Walters began to speak again. So far he had not asked her a single question.

'Each time he was late I feared the worst. I always knew that one day I would have to go through this. Please don't think me callous, but I've been wondering if Dave saw the knife and welcomed it. They told me there'd been no struggle, you see, and that it would have been over very quickly. Still, I suppose they always say that.

'Chief inspector, tell me, was it him? The girl's father?'

With great care Ian placed his cup and saucer on the table. His hand shook and his face felt hot. He was furious with Brenda and with everyone else. What girl? How had he been allowed to come here without all the facts?

51

'Oh, God.' Pat covered her mouth with her hand. 'You don't know, do you? How stupid of me. Why should you have known?' She shook her head. 'Ten years ago Dave started his own business. It was simple. He bought a large van and made urgent deliveries for anyone who required his services. You know the sort of thing; spare parts for garages if their own drivers was busy, packages, stationery, anything really. He covered a large area. Self-employed and a free man, he used to say. Then just over a year ago, on his way back from Market Harborough a child ran out into the road. Dave always used back roads on the return journey whenever possible. He never drank during the week and the police proved the van was totally road-worthy. Their measurements of the skid marks showed he wasn't doing much more than forty. But he never stood a chance. The little girl wasn't used to traffic and someone had left the gate open. There was no case to bring, Dave was completely exonerated. But there was a piece in the *Rickenham Herald*. That was what he couldn't live with. Knowing what he'd done was bad enough, but for everyone else to know was worse. It was a little girl called Alice and although Debbie was older than her, she was a constant reminder of what he had taken from those parents.'

'I see. And you always believed he would take his own life because of this?'

'Yes. I just hope he's finally at peace.' She paused. 'Will I be allowed to see him?'

'Of course.' He had already been identified by staff at the hospital but there were no facial injuries and the post-mortem was not due to take place until the next day. Ian decided to arrange it quickly. He got the impression that now the news had sunk in, Pat Walters would find some sort of peace herself. And it had sunk in, she had used the past tense when speaking of her husband. What she had been anticipating for all those months had finally happened, although not in quite the same way as she had expected.

It was time to ask some questions but first he excused himself and left the room to ring the station from his mobile phone. He wanted to know every detail about that fatal RTA and he wanted the father questioned. But deep down Ian felt certain it was pointless, he would have killed Walters immediately if his anger and grief were too great to contain or he would have taken his

52

revenge slowly. He did not think that a quick knifing would have provided a satisfactory solution. There was, Ian felt, a long way to go.

'What time will you be back?' Jackie asked as she tucked her hair behind her ears then bent to see to one of the children. The question was a formality, she had reached the stage where she hardly cared. Once this, the last child, was born, she was going to see the doctor herself. Danny was such a ditherer. If he'd made up his mind about the vasectomy when they'd discussed it, this latest one wouldn't be on the way.

'Not late,' he said as he pulled on his uniform jacket. They both flinched in recognition of the way things were when he bent to kiss her cheek and missed because one of the children had tugged at her hand and she had turned away. It was purely accidental but indicative of their relationship.

His beat was one of the easier ones and did not, as Jackie believed, often entail unsociable hours. It consisted mostly of residential streets. It was an average sort of area with no real trouble-makers living within its boundaries. On the map it was almost square, covering Deben Lane, Aspen Road, the edge of the Ashleigh Estate and Saxborough Road.

PC Danny Cotton thought of himself as corrupt and felt ashamed. He knew that he would never take a bribe, but what he was doing was somehow worse.

He had almost completed the first circuit of his beat, thinking again how easy it was. Checking shop doors, chatting to the young mums, almost, he thought resignedly, helping old ladies across the road. Then his innermost beliefs took over. What was wrong with helping old ladies across the road? Better that than mugging them, beating them senseless for their pension money or, as it went these days, beating them almost to death just for the hell of it.

He sighed. These were excuses and he knew it. What he had done was to break with everything he had once believed in. And it was too late to go back now.

PC Danny Cotton stared at the houses in Saxborough Road. Three storeys high and each with a basement. Grand old houses once, even he, as a young man, realised that. But now, bed-sit land, apart from one or two. The houses had been built when horses and carriages had paraded up and down; now the wide road had more than its share of white markings, zigzags, bollards and bus-stops. Number 101 was one of the few places to remain intact. There was a reason for that. And Danny Cotton was one of the few people to know what it was. The present owner could afford to keep it that way.

Barbara Fletcher had moved to Rickenham Green three or four years ago. She was, so it was said, something of a socialite. She had certainly joined several clubs. That she was well heeled was beyond question. Apparently her mornings were spent in leisurely pursuits, taking coffee with friends, having her hair done or spending an hour or so in one of the town's three beauty salons. All this she had told him over coffee one morning.

Her age was open to question but from things she let slip on other occasions he assumed she was somewhere in her early fifties. It was not only PC Danny Cotton who thought she looked years younger. She had let it be known that she was a widow and it was generally assumed that her wealth had come from her deceased husband. This was mainly because she had never mentioned having been employed.

She was slim and full-breasted with only a hint of plumpness around the hips. Her nails were painted in pearly shades which matched her lipstick and were well shaped and not too long. Her hair neither fair nor brown, was that intermediate shade which might once have been auburn. She wore it in a perfect French roll with a few loose wisps to soften the effect and to emphasise her enviable cheekbones. Yet so far as he knew Barbara Fletcher did not go out with men.

Despite his now regular visits to the house she remained an enigma. But he had noticed that she was adept at avoiding answering personal questions and there was always, he realised, a hint of laughter in her green eyes.

But PC Danny Cotton was quite shrewd. He had guessed at her background and realised that Barbara had once earned a living from selling her body. But she had been lucky, she was beautiful and had got out before it was too late. She had, presumably, married well, possibly a man from whom she had been able to keep her past. Danny did not know his name. 'She never talks about him,' Emma had said when he had asked her. 'Besides, it's none of my business.'

PC Danny Cotton had a vestige of respect for Barbara Fletcher even though he knew what she was. She had not ended up on drugs or with an unwanted child to support. Whatever she had been in her youth she had managed to convince people that she was a lady.

Danny's problem was that he believed Emma was the answer to his own dreams, a fact he could not come to terms with when he knew he also loved his wife. Emma and Molly, who both worked for Barbara two nights a week, also had daytime jobs.

Danny continued down the tree-lined road. No burglar alarms rang at any of the detached houses, no suspicious characters lurked in gardens and, at this time of year, no windows had been left open. At the end of the road he turned left and left again and came into Saxborough Road. He stopped to chat to a shopkeeper who ran a small general store. 'Terrible business, those murders,' Brian Nicholls commented, sucking his teeth in his habitual manner.

'Yes.'

'Ah, can't talk about it. I understand. Just tell me to mind my own business.' He laughed. 'Talk about wit. Mind my own business? Get it? Still, the weather's on the mend. Shan't be sorry when it's spring.'

Danny let him ramble on. Brian could speak for ten minutes without interruption. His silent assessment of Barbara continued. He needed to know exactly what he was up against. The clubs and societies to which she belonged were not joined solely for her enjoyment but to single out the men as potential clients. Danny realised he was no better than those faceless men: worse, probably, because he wasn't even paying for it. And Emma had told him the services did not come cheaply. Three figures? he wondered. Yes, probably.

Only in retrospect could he see what had happened. Barbara Fletcher was a single woman living in a large house. Had she had a stream of single men knocking at the door it might have raised an eyebrow or two under any circumstances. But Saxborough Road was ideal. Bed-sit land. An area of transient neighbours who had far more on their minds than what was happening at number 101, which was why, until it was virtually pointed out to him, he had not recognised what was going on. By then it was too late.

Emma, who worked in a sandwich bar by day, told him that she earned more from two nights at Barbara's than from her full-time job. Molly, the other girl, apparently worked in a boutique. I've never given much thought to money, he realised, other than having enough to get by on. And that's going to be harder when the next baby comes. But to Emma it represented the answer to whatever dreams she possessed.

'Don't you care?' he had asked her. 'How can you do this? All those men?'

'There aren't that many,' she told him in a matter-of-fact tone of voice as if that made it all right.

'What about me?'

'What about you, Danny?'

'You know how I feel. And those men are married, they have families . . .' He had stopped then, knowing how hypocritical he was being. But surely it was different, he loved Emma. It gave him a headache thinking about it. He loved Jackie, too.

The last time he had seen Emma she had said without any preliminaries, 'Look, Danny, let's get one thing straight. These men may be married but they can afford to pay for what they want and this way is far better than them having affairs which can lead to more involvement than they anticipated, possibly the break-up of the marriage. Besides, a satisfied man makes a better husband, and the wives don't know.'

He was just beginning to see that her comments were not necessarily a defence of her actions but more likely a warning to him.

Danny now knew from things Emma had said that the men arrived discreetly, never more than one at a time and never on nights other than Tuesdays and Thursdays. They handed over their money, were given drinks served by Barbara herself and were then shown upstairs. This, he gathered, was the cause of her constant, secret mirth. These were the men with whom she socialised, along with their wives. What a danger she posed. And he, a police officer, had fallen into her trap and become hooked.

*

56

Barbara Fletcher had taken every possible precaution to keep her dealings out of the public eye. Because of the limitations of what she was doing, it would be very hard to prove anything. Even so she had had a fright when her cleaning woman had announced the presence of one of the local constabulary on a dreary day some months ago. In a flash her dreams disappeared. Self-control returned immediately she summed up the young PC who stood in her drawing-room, his helmet clutched awkwardly to his side.

'Do sit down,' Barbara had said in her melodious voice. 'May I get you something? Tea or coffee?'

PC Cotton had accepted the offer of a cup of coffee and made himself at home in the deep cushions of one of the three large settees. When he had drunk the coffee Barbara showed him around the house, by that time realising that if anything had been suspected the police would have come at night. Danny Cotton, local beat bobby, had simply come to introduce himself and to offer advice if required. It was all part of the new image of the police service, he told her.

She had smiled benevolently when PC Cotton expressed his approval of her security arrangements: smoke alarms on each landing, locks on all the windows and strong bolts and locks on back and front doors. 'Living alone one can't be too careful. Thank you so much for calling in,' Barbara had said as she showed him out. 'I'm almost always here in the afternoons – come and have a cup of tea whenever you have the time.'

When he had left Barbara leant against the front door and grinned. She knew already that she had him. His face had told her everything she needed to know long before his afternoon visits became regular and she had heard about the three children and the fourth on the way. His despair was obvious, as was his desire for something other than what fate had dealt out to him. And no harm could come of having a policeman on her side.

But now she was worried. She had gradually introduced the name of Emma, the less aggressively beautiful of the two girls, into conversations as her niece, and Danny had taken the bait. Emma, she had hinted, was, like himself, unhappy. 'I have never seen the harm in two miserable people giving each other a little happiness as long as it doesn't hurt anyone else,' she had confided shyly to him. 'Would you like to meet her?'

His biggest mistake had been to say yes. Danny had been

puzzled, aware that Barbara was trying to fix him up with a woman. It had taken him several meetings with Emma, all of which had taken place at Barbara's, before he realised he had been set up. He, of all people, should have been suspicious. It was only when he had seen a total stranger, a man roughly his own age, emerging from a bedroom some way down the corridor that he realised what was going on – as, he suspected, Barbara had meant him to do. That man had been De Quincy. He could not report any of what he knew without breaking up his marriage and possibly losing his job. Who would believe that he had been using the services of a prostitute, of a brothel, without payment and without realising what he was doing until it was too late? And hadn't he, deep down, shut his eyes to the possibility of what was going on there? There was also the added complication of Emma herself. He had now taken to meeting her at her flat. The thought of not seeing her again made him feel sick.

Barbara had guessed at all this, but Emma was no fool. It was time Danny Cotton was given his marching orders. And it would be so much easier from Emma's flat because it distanced him from her own concerns. She would speak to her about it soon. PC Cotton was no threat.

Jackie Cotton was numb. Life and the children had reduced her to that state. Danny was up to something but she was not sure what. If it was illegal and he lost his job she could not imagine what would happen to them. 'We'll end up with nothing,' she told the middle child who was being particularly clinging that day but who was too young to understand what his mother was saying.

If it was an affair, she believed she could cope with that as long as he kept up the payments on the house and the other things. But if it was an affair, why wasn't he more cheerful? Corruption. The word kept creeping into her head. Had he got himself involved in something from which there was no escape? I can't think about it, I mustn't, she told herself, knowing that the children needed their lunch. There was no one in whom she could confide. Since the third child was born there had been no time for friends and her family lived too far away. Her parents

58

were good, decent people and admired the job their son-in-law did. They would not understand her worries, especially as she always wrote to say how well they were all doing and enclosed happy snapshots of the children.

Three boys within four and a half years; Robert, Ellis and Louis. The choice of names had been hers. How she prayed this last child would be a girl.

She took a perverse kind of comfort from the fact that two men had been murdered. Danny never discussed his work and he refused to allow her to mention it. He insisted upon keeping his home life as a separate entity. But if he was involved in these cases it would go some way towards explaining his mood and why he was doing so much overtime.

'Hungry, Mummy,' Robert insisted, tugging at the hem of her maternity dress.

'Me, hungry,' Ellis chipped in, still at the stage of emulating everything his older brother did. The baby set up a wail and, fighting off despair, Jackie went to the kitchen to prepare their meals. If only it was warmer and they could play outside, she thought, I might be able to read for an hour. The house was modern but small. In front the design was open-plan; a small rectangle of grass was divided from the neighbours' similar patches by a single chain-link strung between six-inch white posts. But the back garden, although also small, was surrounded by a high creosoted fence and the tall gate had a latch which none of them could yet reach.

As she bent stiffly to get milk from the fridge, her eye caught the calendar on the wall. Her next hospital appointment was in two days' time. 'I'll ask the consultant,' she said, quite used to speaking aloud to herself. 'I'll see if they can sterilise me the minute the baby's born.' She was sure she had heard it was possible. Then she frowned as she looked at Danny's writing. His shifts were clearly marked. He had worked two early shifts at the weekend but he had been out when those men were killed. On Sunday he had come home on time, as he had promised, and they had shared a late lunch. Danny had offered to take the children out to give her a break but the youngest needed a nap and was sniffling and she thought it was too cold to take the other two out and risk them coming down with something. But

Danny had gone out anyway, saying he needed some air. That was at three thirty. He had not returned until six. And the second man had been killed during that interval.

'Oh, no.' Jackie slumped into the only vacant kitchen chair. Three pairs of worried eyes watched her. Was it possible that Danny had killed those men? And all those other times, where had he been? If he really had worked extra hours his pay packet would prove it. But that overtime would not be included at the end of this month, it was always one month in arrears. How could she wait that long to find out? Asking him was impossible and the idea of speaking to his sergeant was totally impossible.

She shook her head and managed a smile for the three silent children. This pregnancy, she thought, is turning my brain.

'We need to find him.' Ian was worried. There had been several more reports of a large man behaving in a peculiar manner. One woman had encountered him in Bradley Road. She had crossed over quickly because she thought he might have been carrying a knife. 'He was ranting and raving. Shouldn't be allowed on the streets,' she had commented indignantly.

The following two calls which appeared to concern this same person were from worried householders. One claimed the man had been sitting on his front garden wall talking to himself, the other that the man was standing beneath a tree waving a knife around. Could it be their man? A nutter with nothing to gain? Ian wanted to know. But once again the man seemed to have disappeared into thin air.

'The description doesn't match anyone we know,' the duty sergeant had explained to Ian. 'The lads out there are pretty good, they tend to get to know them all.'

'Thanks. Keep looking,' Ian said. He was puzzled. If it was their man he wasn't exactly hiding and why, if he was wielding a knife, hadn't he struck again?

'Don't tempt fate,' Short said, when Ian pointed this out to him.

5

'Matthew and Karen Collinson,' Inspector Short said as he smoothed down the strands of hair across his scalp. 'Only the one child at the time but they've recently had another. Moved away six months after the accident. Couldn't stand being able to see from their front window the spot where the little girl was killed. Living in Derbyshire now. Absolutely no chance of either of them having killed Walters.'

DCI Roper nodded. He did not ask for alibis. If Short said absolutely no chance, then that was a fact of life. Besides, Ian had not really believed that the father of little Alice Collinson was guilty.

'Also,' Short continued, beaming round at the assembled detectives as if he found his next piece of news amusing, 'according to the Met, Charlotte Jones is doing her nut. Claims to know nothing about Anne Morrisson and says she's coming up here to scratch her eyes out, or words to that effect. Hardly the attitude of the recently bereaved, but we're all different. However, we have to consider that one or other of these women might be lying, that they might have known about the other. Nah, forget it.' John Short sucked irritably at his moustache.

'Go on.' Ian sat at a desk, tapping a pencil against its edge. It was late on Monday afternoon and the building, like all the others that could be seen from the windows, was ablaze with lights. In the High Street the ceremony of switching on the Christmas lights would be taking place in a few hours' time. Uniformed men had been deployed to divert the traffic and to make their presence known amongst the crowds where, at this time of year in particular, opportunist thieves would be out in force hoping to find undone handbags with purses visible and shopping left on the back seats of cars. Such matters were not Ian's concern but they still angered him. The public were stupid for not acting more carefully, and the thieves despicable for ruining people's Christmases.

'Sir?' Brenda Gibbons, arms folded, her hair gleaming under

the overhead lights, leaned against the wall between two windows. She was staring at him.

'Nothing.' He was aware that he had been grinning inanely, laughing at himself. Moira was right. Even in his own head he was beginning to sound like his father. His thoughts had been about to travel along the lines of 'In my day we were able to go out and leave our doors unlocked.'

'May I?' Inspector Short glanced cynically around the room, baffled by the undercurrents. The only one who seemed to be paying any attention was DC Alan Campbell. But who knows, he thought, Markham, who was gazing out of the window at the street below, might also have been listening. To Short, who thought and spoke in clichés, Markham was more likely away with the fairies. 'If Elizabeth Smith's statement is true, then the perp was male in De Quincy's case. It's unlikely one of these women disguised herself as a man and then chose that method of getting rid of her unfaithful lover. Nor is it the usual modus operandi of your average hit man, supposing one of them hired someone else to do the job. Wrong place, wrong time of day, wrong method. And whoever wielded that spanner was, according to the PM, taller than De Quincy. I think we can, with reservations, rule his two women out.'

'Yes.' Ian nodded in agreement. Charlotte Jones had been with her parents in Devon, where she went most weekends, believing that De Quincy had returned to his parental home in Suffolk. Other people's lives fascinated Ian. How could it be that two people lived together but did not introduce each other to their own familes?

Anne Morrisson, he recalled, had told a WPC she had been preparing a special dinner and there was much evidence of this when the news had been broken. Not a perfect alibi, of course, and she had been on the spot, but Anne Morrisson was shorter than Justin De Quincy. I must ring Moira, Ian thought, remembering the many meals she had taken trouble over which had gone to waste. And there wasn't much more that could be done that day. The post-mortem on David Walters was to take place in the morning. Pat Walters, with an escort, had already been taken to view the body.

Forensics were working on clothing and on both the spanner

and the knife, which had been left in the body. In both cases the murder weapon had been left at the scene. Ian wondered if something so trivial could be a connection. No fingerprints on either which, to everyone's mind, suggested both killings had been premeditated. The implements were the sort which could have been bought anywhere and it was, in a way, clever of the killer not to have taken them with him. They would have had to have been disposed of somewhere and that might have led the police to him. It also prevented unnecessary traces of blood or evidence leaving the scene with him. The scarves and the method convinced Ian that this was the work of a man.

They were now in possession of three lists made out by each of the women who had lived with the victims, and many of the people on them had yet to be interviewed. So far nothing adverse had come to light regarding the two men's working lives. It could wait. Ian picked up the phone and dialled his own number to tell Moira that he would be early and that, with a bit of luck, he'd get the bathroom finished by bedtime. He had discovered that the action of painting and the sight of a pristine expanse of wall were both soothing and satisfying. There was no reply.

Even outside the police station, which was in a road off the High Street, there was a buzz of excitement and more pedestrians than usual. Ian pulled out of the car-park and made a right turn, only to be thwarted at the top of the road by the red and white police barriers and a uniformed officer. 'Bloody Christmas lights,' he muttered, catching a glimpse of the crowds already lining the streets as he indicated to make a detour. He hated Christmas but realised Moira would make an effort this year as Mark would be home.

There was a snarl-up in Saxborough Road as people from the outlying villages made their way into Rickenham for the annual spectacle. Begrudgingly, Ian admitted that the Chamber of Commerce always put on a good show with their illuminations.

Finally parked in Belmont Terrace, although some way from his own house, Ian felt more cheerful at the thought of spending the evening with Moira. 'Terrace' wasn't technically the correct word to describe where they lived. Each side of the street consisted of three blocks of seven houses. The Ropers' house was at the end of the second block and could, in reality, be described as semi-detached. But no lights shone from the windows. Even when Moira was in the kitchen there was a faint glow from behind the coloured glass of the fanlight.

He walked the few steps from the gate to the narrow path which ran up to the door, along the front and around the side of the house. The small garden facing the street held only a couple of evergreen shrubs. The kitchen door was at the back and the one they both used most frequently. The back garden was Moira's terrain. During the many years they had lived in the house she had turned a wilderness into a thriving, productive piece of land. Both flowers and vegetables flourished, according to the time of year. Ian's only participation had been to hold the slabs whilst their next-door neighbour had dealt with sand and cement and built them a small patio upon which he sat on summer evenings with a cold beer in his hand and surveyed the work of his wife. Those days were still a long way off. It was dark and cold but at least the temperature had risen above freezing. He pursed his lips and, head on one side, wondered if he might have a bash at gardening himself. For years Moira had been warning him that he ought to have a hobby, that if he didn't take up something soon he would be bored senseless when he retired. But now he had a sneaking suspicion that he might have lots of them, that he might be like his father, now long dead, who threw himself into one activity after another but never stuck with any of them.

He retrieved the daily paper from the front door mat and frowned. Moira had not been home since she had finished work or it would have been on the kitchen table and in an untidy state. She had never been able to refold a newspaper properly. He made tea, a strong mugful, and took off his jacket. He slipped an old cardigan over his working clothes, then, with a sigh of pleasure, he removed the lid of the paint tin with a knife from the kitchen drawer, hoping Moira would not notice he had bent it, retrieved the brush from its jar of water and went upstairs to start work.

Markham had managed to avoid John Short for most of the day. It was a relief to both men. Already tempers were not so easily held in check. It was a bad sign so early in the investigations.

On his way out he caught sight of Brenda Gibbons chatting to a WPC. She had her coat on. 'Got time for a drink?'

Brenda did not hesitate. 'Yep.' Anything was better than going home. On her next day off she was going to speak to the mortgage people. A quick telephone call had ascertained that negative equity did not mean the end of her hopes. An arrangement could be made for a one hundred per cent mortgage with any arrears to be added to the new mortgage once the hideous house had been sold. It was reason enough to celebrate.

She hurried up the road trying to keep up with Markham and wondered if he would manage to bring himself to make conversation.

Without asking where she'd like to go, he took her to the Three Feathers in the High Street and ordered her drink. 'Do you know Richie Andrews?' he asked as he handed her a Campari and soda.

Brenda shook her head and frowned. The name rang a vague bell but she couldn't place him. 'Why? What's he done?'

'Nothing. That's the point. One arrest on a charge of breaking and entering, nothing since.'

'Perhaps he's gone straight. Yes, all right, I know about proverbial pigs.'

'He's a loner, and he doesn't frequent pubs.'

'Not totally like you then, Markham. You have been known to shift the odd pint or two. Can I ask you something? Don't you get pissed off with your own company?'

'Often. Which is why I don't inflict it on anyone else.'

What is this? Brenda thought. Markham in what for him passes for a heart-to-heart? But did she dare question him further? She decided she did. 'No girlfriend?'

'No.' He turned away so she could not see his face.

'I'm sorry. It's none of my business. Call it female curiosity. I don't know why women always want to know these things.' She knew that his parents were dead, that he had been born to them late and that they had been poor and tired out. She sensed that there had been someone in Markham's life. He was the sort of man who, if he made a commitment, would make it for life. Then she remembered. Richie Andrews, another loner, had lost his friend in a car crash. His only friend. Surely the impartial, emotionless DS Markham wasn't making comparisons? But he wouldn't have brought up the name unless he really wanted to know.

'There have been women. I seem to recall taking you out once.'

Brenda grinned. 'It was hardly a night of unleashed passion, if you don't mind me mentioning it. A pizza and a bottle of house wine and I was left to make my own way home.'

'That's more than most get.'

'Most? Come on, tell me, how many have there been?'

'That, Constable Gibbons, really is none of your business.'

Oh, shit, she thought. For once I thought I was getting close to him. I thought we were actually going to have a reasonable conversation. Her face was hot; to cover her embarrassment she asked about Richard Andrews.

'Yes, I thought that's who he was,' she said when Markham had recounted the story. 'But why your interest now? Look, it's more likely that the shock of Cooper's death was enough to put him off crime for ever.'

'Maybe. But why stay here? Surely he'd want to distance himself from those memories?'

Ah, she thought, so that's what brought you to Rickenham from Nottingham. According to the Chief, Markham had been with them for about ten years. He was now in his middle to late thirties. Had he, ten years ago, suffered a loss which caused him to move? There was no way she could ask without a worse rebuff than she had already received. It was strange, she gave little thought to the man. Markham was Markham. That's how most people viewed him, forgetting that he was also a fellow human being. One day, maybe, the barriers would come down. It would be very interesting to discover what lay behind the façade. 'My turn,' she said, reaching into her handbag for her purse. One more drink then she would go home and start clearing out drawers and cupboards. Very soon she would know if it was possible to return to the welcome sight of a For Sale board outside the house.

Elizabeth Smith stood staring out of her window at the spot where Justin De Quincy had been killed. She had to crane her neck to do so but it fascinated her. Only then did she wish she had a confidante, someone she could go over all the details with time and time again. Since it had happened she could think of nothing else. Oddly, the fact of it occurring almost on her doorstep did not cause her any anxiety. The people involved were nothing to do with her and they were not like the noisy crowds she had to endure on match days.

Because there was no one to talk to she rang the number on the card DS Markham had given her.

'I've remembered something,' she told him when he came to the phone. 'The one who ran away, he had a moustache. I just caught a glimpse of it. Do you need me to come down and make a new statement?'

'No, that won't be necessary,' Markham told her. 'And thank you for letting us know.'

The conversation was short and Elizabeth was dissatisfied. Didn't they realise how important that piece of information was? And she was a witness, the only one as far as she could make out from gossip she had overheard in the shops. Although desperate for an audience she refused to discuss it with her neighbours. It serves them right, she thought, they've never made much attempt to speak to me before.

Half-past six. It was time for supper. Tonight there was cold ham, left over from the joint she had cooked for Sunday lunch and which seemed to be lasting for ever. There were also mashed potatoes and tinned peas. To liven it up a bit she had bought a packet of onion sauce mix.

As she ate her solitary meal Elizabeth paused every so often to recapture the events of Saturday evening. If only people knew how important she was to the case. If only she could think of a way to be of even more help.

The scene, played so many times in her head, had taken on a reality of its own. She now saw everything that had happened, not just the two men then the single running figure. How clearly the man's hand registered in her mind as he raised it to strike the first blow, how awful the look in his eyes as he brought it down again. Green eyes, surely. The potatoes were almost cold by then but Elizabeth did not believe in waste. She ate them anyway then took her plate to the kitchen to wash it before making tea.

She had watched very little television since Saturday, except for the news, but she had since discovered that the murder, along with that of a second man, was receiving more coverage on the local radio station which she now left on all the time.

She could hardly wait for Friday's edition of the *Rickenham Herald* which would cover the story in detail and might even mention her name. Perhaps she ought to make sure it did by giving them a ring and asking if they were interested in her personal story.

She retrieved the previous week's issue from the bag containing old newspapers which she took down to the recycling bins in the car-park once a week and found the name of the editor. She thought it best to go straight to the top.

'Is that you, love?' Ian called from upstairs.

'Yes.' Moira raised her eyebrows as she answered his unnecessary question. For who else would be letting themselves in with a key?

'Don't come up.'

She smiled. He's nearly finished the bathroom, she thought, amazed that his enthusiasm had not waned the moment he had gone back to work. Rather than tire him further, his new interest seemed to be rejuvenating him. Which is no bad thing, she told herself. He had a tendency to harp on about the old days and a pessimistic view of the future. Let it last, she prayed, whilst wondering what would happen when all the rooms had been redecorated.

'I didn't intend to be so late. I watched the lights being switched on. It wasn't worth coming home first and, to be honest, I didn't expect to find you here yet,' she said when he came downstairs with the paintbrush held carefully over the almost empty tin.

Ian kissed her cheek on his way to the sink. 'Now, come and have a look.'

Moira stood in the bathroom door and surveyed his handiwork. It was a mistake. It was hideous. Against the stark white tiles the palest of apple greens looked much darker than the tiny rectangle on the chart from which they had chosen it. 'You've done a wonderful job, Ian. And I still can't believe it.' It was true. There were no paint splashes on the bathroom suite or the floor. But the colour was awful. How could she live with it? Easily

68

solved, she realised. If Ian retains his interest I can get him to redo it in a few months' time.

'I knew you'd like it.' Ian grinned. 'What's for supper?'

He hadn't noticed the disappointment she had tried to hide. 'I hadn't really thought about it. Something quick. Pasta?'

'That's fine.'

'I got a few bits and pieces for Christmas in my lunch hour. Don't worry, I'm not doing the whole bit, I know we agreed to give that up years ago. It's just that I want to make it nice for Mark. At least he'll have his new room to come home to.'

Ian knew what was bothering her. Moira missed their son badly and desperately wanted to make his stay enjoyable and memorable, but without upsetting Ian who hated the whole festive season and all that went with it. Given his own way he would have cancelled it. It was Moira who had to make the compromises, to make it work for him and Mark, and who, by having to do so, would end up enjoying it less than anyone. 'When's he arriving? I know you did tell me,' he added hurriedly, 'but with what's on at work at the moment . . .'

'Yes, I know. He's staying a couple of nights with friends in London then coming on up here at the weekend.'

'Look, don't bother to cook tonight. I am supposed to be on leave. Let me take you out.'

Moira hesitated. It was tempting. 'No. Not tonight. Rickenham's heaving and I bet the restaurants are fully booked by people coming into town for the lights and making a night of it. I wonder why they always choose a Monday?'

Ian had no idea, the thought hadn't crossed his mind. Perhaps it was traditional to switch on the lights that particular day of the week. He watched Moira as she put together a meal. Things were so different from the days when Mark was a boy and she was content to stay at home. Ian could never fault her attributes as a wife and mother or as a woman, but her days of being a slave to the house and the two males with whom she had shared it had long gone. Once she had taken a job her interest in cooking everything from scratch had waned, apart from at weekends when she still went all out in the kitchen. What had surprised him more than anything was that, as young and lovely as she had always looked, working full time had enhanced her in some way. Life really wasn't fair. Even now, although he could see she was tired, her movements were graceful and her neat features composed.

'Shall I make the coffee?' Ian asked when they had finished eating.

'Yes, please.' Moira stacked the dishwasher then straightened up, watching her husband's back as she untied her hair and let it fall free around her shoulders. How well she knew him, how familiar were the plain trousers of which he had several pairs for work because all his shirts, either white or pastel shades, went with them. Today's was a biscuit colour with a brown tie, now loosened. The subtle brown and green dog-tooth check jacket which she had chosen for him hung over the back of a chair. She, too, had noticed that the grey at his temples had begun to spread but would never comment on it. Ian could be quite vain at times. He should have been at home resting; instead he had been called in because they were short-staffed – but when weren't they? she thought – to help with a double murder. And now he was making her coffee.

She took a couple of steps across the kitchen and touched his arm gently. 'Here, you sit down. I'll do it.'

Ian did not, as she had anticipated, pick up the paper and go through to the living-room. He resumed his seat at the table and pushed the salt and pepper grinders around as though they were chess pieces.

Moira almost relented and took out the sugar bowl but shut the cupboard quickly and placed sweeteners and skimmed milk on the table, then the cups and saucers and the coffee pot. 'That bad?' she asked, reading his expression correctly.

Ian nodded. Earlier, watching the bathroom walls take on their new hue, he had been able to forget about work. 'About as bad as it can get. No obvious motive in either case.' He knew he could trust Moira when it came to discussing cases. Gradually he had come to learn that she was a good sounding-board; because she viewed what he told her both objectively and from a distance she was sometimes able to express useful opinions.

'Are they connected?' Moira poured the coffee and sat down. They had always eaten in the kitchen. It was rarely that they entertained guests for whom the dining-room, now Moira's sewing room, needed to be cleared out. Doc Harris and his wife,

70

Shirley, their most regular visitors, were happy to share the informality of mealtimes when they came.

'You may well ask.' Ian told her how little the cases had in common.

'It seems very strange, two in two days. Weren't you worried there'd be a third?'

The kitchen was warm and retained the smell of garlic, now faintly overridden by the aroma of ground coffee. Ian began to relax. He reached behind him for the ashtray and lit a cigarette. Forever unsuccessful in giving up totally, he had finally decided to stick with allocating himself a limited number each day.

They both jumped when the back door gave a loud, unexpected rattle.

'It's just the wind,' Moira commented. 'It must be getting stronger again. At least it's not so cold now. I didn't envy your colleagues, standing around for hours at a time in the freezing cold two days in a row,' she said casually.

It was only later, in bed, that the import of Moira's words struck him. It was another connection. Both men had been killed out of doors. Markham had suggested that the killer was local, but did this mean that he knew both victims? Did he know that they had families at home and therefore he could not kill them there? How typical of Moira to have picked on something so obvious no one else had noticed it. He turned on his side and wrapped an arm around her. She responded by moving a little but Ian knew she was already asleep.

If it is one man, then who, and why? And who and where was the large, knife-wielding person they kept hearing about but seemed unable to find? Was he the murderer, insane, unafraid to show himself, yet still elusive? Elizabeth Smith had said nothing about either of the men she had seen being large. Ian fell asleep with many unanswerable questions on his mind, not least of which was how would he and Mark get on over Christmas when they would be confined to the house for longer periods than usual?

Markham put down the phone. Elizabeth Smith was far from senile and he had guessed that, given time, she would remember more than she had thought possible at first. A moustache. That certainly narrowed things down. Except, if the man suspected he had been seen, he might have shaved it off. And in that case, Markham thought, people who knew him would notice and he would draw more attention to himself. If he was clever he would leave well alone. He made a note of the conversation and passed the information on.

The Chief had gone home but Alan Campbell was still feeding the computer which was, as ever, as hungry for information as Campbell was for food. Short was nowhere to be seen and if he had left had not said goodnight. Brenda Gibbons was combing her hair and checking her face in her handbag mirror. Markham grinned his sharp-toothed grin. 'You seeing our prime suspect tonight?'

'None of your business, Markham,' she said, in retaliation for the previous night. She turned her back and sprayed on perfume. The remarks of her male colleagues no longer made her blush. Thankfully Andrew Osborne had been cleared of any involvement in the De Quincy case. She was seeing Andrew, and it was some time since they had managed a whole night out together. On the most recent occasions when she had been free he had been away on protracted court cases.

'See you,' Markham said, and swung from the room.

It suddenly struck Brenda that, as fearsome as he could be, as silent and threatening and powerful as he was, Markham had never made a crude remark in her presence. 'He has to have something in his favour, I suppose,' she muttered as she pulled on her heavy coat.

Markham had already reached the end of the road and was turning into the High Street. His loping walk carried him there quickly. This was what he liked best. Being out there, speaking to people. Tonight he would question everyone he knew; casually and with no hint of what he really wanted to know. He would not make a single reference to the two men who had been killed. He wanted information, nothing specific, just any information at all. Specific questions, he had discovered, only brought about a state of muteness.

Down the length of the High Street sweet-faced angels and jolly Father Christmases twinkled as they swayed wildly in the increasing wind. In shop windows gifts and toys and expensive food items were displayed; a mixture of the religious, the commercial and the pagan sides of Christmas. Markham ignored them all.

He reached Saxborough Road, occasionally having to shoulder his way through the dispersing crowds who had come to see the lights and take advantage of the evening's late night shopping. They were now making their way home. The mayor had made his short speech and some minor celebrity from the local radio station had thrown the switch. The fun was over and the police were removing the barriers which had held back the traffic.

The lights of the Black Horse were more welcoming to Markham than anything suspended overhead. He pushed open the door and a rush of beery warmth greeted him. As always, the air was heavy with smoke which hung in clouds beneath the stained lamp fittings. A cocktail of sound enveloped him. It consisted of noisy conversation, the clack of pool balls and music from the juke-box which competed with the raucus theme tunes from the fruit machines. To Markham this was simply background to which he was oblivious as he scanned the room. He had a gut feeling that the killer, and he was sure it was one man, was a loner. The people who used the Black Horse were the opposite; they seemed unable to function as single units and because of this they were the first to notice anyone who stood out by being solitary, a state which was beyond their comprehension.

The landlord had seen him enter and was already pouring his drink. Markham was all right as far as the police went. He wiped his hands down the sides of the open cardigan which he wore over a grubby shirt whose buttons strained across his enormous gut, plucked at his unkempt beard then said good evening as he slid Markham's pint across the sopping wet surface of the counter.

Markham handed over the correct money which earned him a smile from the thick red lips almost hidden by the full beard. The landlord shook his head. Markham took this to mean that no strangers had been in lately and that he hadn't heard of anything untoward taking place in the area.

So sure he had been about to learn something, Markham left after an hour and several desultory conversations with the customers he knew but would never dream of socialising with. Walking back to the self-contained flat where he had lived alone for the past nine years, he caught sight of a figure he recognised. It was Richie Andrews.

Richie Andrews was smartly dressed, as he had been on the other occasions Markham had seen him. Perhaps he had maligned him, maybe he really had got himself a job and settled down. But Markham doubted it. He was not in the right frame of mind to challenge him now. His conversation with Brenda Gibbons which had taken place in the Three Feathers had unsettled him more than he had realised. It was not her fault and he had treated her no differently from usual today. But he had foolishly believed those memories were safely locked away. Now, because of a few careless words, they had risen to the surface.

Markham let himself into his flat, locked the door and sat down. 'Oh, God, Julie. I still miss you,' he said to the empty room.

6

'May I speak to Martyn Bright, please?' Elizabeth Smith asked the young woman on the switchboard of the *Rickenham Herald* first thing on Tuesday morning.

'Who's calling?'

She hesitated before giving her name. She had had no dealings with the press before, not even by way of placing an advert in their classified pages. Suddenly decisive, she said who she was. Mr Bright might know her name already if the police had issued a statement. She was put through immediately, not realising how lucky she was because Martyn Bright was normally a very busy man.

'And so,' she concluded, having given him the outline of the story, 'I am in possession of all these details and the police don't want to know. I thought if you printed them then someone might come forward who could identify the man. This monster.' For he had become so in Elizabeth's eyes, growing in stature daily, his eyes no longer green but steely grey. His forehead was low and his eyes were too close together. She could not see that she had formed a mental identikit using all the features her mother had

74

told her to beware of in men. 'Naturally I don't expect any payment,' she added, aware of the silence at the other end of the line. Perhaps Mr Bright had expected her to name a sum before imparting the information. It did not cross her mind that the local paper offered no remuneration except to its staff: she associated every newspaper with the stories she had read about people being paid large amounts of money for telling all.

'Thank you for calling us, Mrs Smith, but I'm afraid we'll be unable to use your story without the consent of the CID.'

'Well! Really!' she said, hurt and offended, when she had replaced the receiver. 'No wonder the country's in the state it's in.'

As the day wore on she became irritated then angry, fuming at the injustice done to her. She was a decent, law-abiding citizen who had done more than her duty and she had been rejected out of hand by both the police and the press. Sitting at her table in the window, she began to compose a letter of complaint outlining the inefficiency of the Rickenham police which she would send to her MP, a copy of which would go to the *Herald*.

Martyn Bright did not replace his own receiver, he simply depressed the disconnecting button and and rang Ian Roper, insisting that he spoke to him because what he had to say was important. Everyone at the station knew who he was and he would not have been put through if he was just fishing.

'Yes, Martyn?' Ian answered abruptly. A press release had been issued, worded carefully so as to reveal very little. Bright, now he had matured, understood the way in which things worked, therefore Ian was surprised to hear from him at this stage.

'I know you're busy but I had some woman on the phone claiming she can give a clear account of all that happened when De Quincy copped it. She also says you're not prepared to listen.'

'What?'

'She gave her name as Elizabeth Smith.'

'It's her real name.' What was the woman up to? Markham had found her to be a reliable witness and she had even rung back when she recalled the moustache. He groaned as he saw how it might be. If there was a moustache, he thought.

'Obviously we're ignoring it,' Bright continued, although he had no need to state the fact. He would have been out of business if he had printed confidential police information.

75

'And well you might. This is off the record, but all she saw was two men and their shadows, and then very briefly.'

Well, I thought you'd want to know. Can I expect anything else by Thursday lunchtime?'

'Go ahead and print what we've given you. If there's anything new the press officer'll be in touch.' About to hang up, Ian realised he was once more taking out his frustrations on someone who did not deserve it, someone, in fact, who had done him a favour by warning him of what Mrs Smith might be capable. 'Thanks, Martyn. I owe you one.'

Brenda Gibbons was despatched to Alma Road. Elizabeth Smith must be warned of the dangers of her inventions. She was jeopardising both the case and her own safety. No doubt she wished to see her name in lights but to advertise in the local paper or anywhere else it might be seen or heard that she could describe the murderer accurately was asking for trouble even if she was lying. But they did need to know if either of the men she had seen was unduly large. Calls were still coming in about someone making a nuisance of himself.

Brenda's brief visit to Alma Road was unproductive. Unlike Markham and WPC Blount before her, she was not offered a cup of tea. Still, she thought wryly, it would not have been comfortable drinking it on the front doorstep. She had not been invited in.

'I have nothing further to add,' Elizabeth Smith said acidly. 'Any vital information I might have given you is now locked safely in my head for ever.

'And you might as well know, I'm beginning to believe some of the awful things people say about the police. Now, if you'll excuse me, I'm rather busy.'

Brenda tried to placate her, to warn her of the dangers of saying too much to the wrong people, but Elizabeth's ears seemed to be clamped shut as tightly as her mouth had become once she had said her piece.

The early morning weather forecast had predicted yet another rise in the temperature. Shivering on that scrubbed doorstep, Brenda doubted if this could possibly be true. The wind seemed to penetrate the tiniest gaps in her winter clothing. What worried her most was the possibility that Mrs Smith really had seen more than she had recalled originally or, conversely, whether the reverse was true and she had lied about the moustache. Her telephoning Martyn Bright suggested that what may have amounted to the only bit of excitement in her life had turned her into an attention-seeker. The case was becoming more complicated by the minute.

Grateful for the shelter of the car, Brenda shut the door and started the engine. She was to pick up Alan Campbell then they were going to speak to Anne Morrisson and Pat Walters again. She was aware of Elizabeth Smith's rigid figure watching from the window as she made a faultless three-point turn and drove off. Not too busy to make sure I've gone, Brenda noticed.

Markham had been surprised to discover that Richie Andrews had not moved from the flat in Saxborough Road that he had shared with Cooper. Johnny Vaughan, for reasons of his own, had lived elsewhere. No, not for reasons of his own. Andrews and Cooper wouldn't have wanted him with them. Markham did not doubt that their friendship was platonic, albeit unusually close. Their past history revealed no homosexual tendencies and, according to their social reports, their relationship had been described as brotherly by those teachers who had remembered them.

He had no excuse for going to see him; Richie was neither a suspect nor a witness in any active case. Markham, who rarely stopped to analyse his reasons for doing anything, just knew that he wanted to speak to him because something deep down in his subconscious dictated that he did so. He only wished he knew what it was. It would have to wait until he was off duty, there were greater priorities to be dealt with first. Late on Wednesday afternoon he went to join the others at the end of what had turned out to be an uneventful day.

'She's in a terrible state,' Brenda said. 'At least the sister's there and she seems like a sensible woman. It's odd, Anne took it reasonably calmly when I originally broke the news about Charlotte Jones, but she's had a couple of days for it to sink in and it's really got to her.' How do men get away with it? Brenda wondered. It was not a sexist thought, it was virtually impossible for women to act as a wife to two men without one of them knowing about it. What had happened to Anne Morrisson was far more common than many people supposed. 'However, she's certain there's nothing more she can add. De Quincy didn't seem worried about anything and had not acted any differently over the past few months. She's convinced it was just a mindless killing.'

'Aren't they all?' Ian commented with feeling.

'There is one other thing . . .' Brenda paused. 'The house which she told me they were buying together, well, it seems De Quincy hasn't been making his share of the payments for some time. Fortunately Anne bought it through the estate agency she works for and she got a good deal and can afford the repayments on her own. De Quincy's half now belongs to her but there aren't any life policies, it seems.'

'You mean she's now got to continue to cover his share?'

'Yes.' Brenda looked glum. Initially it seemed that she and Anne Morrisson had nothing whatsoever in common. With each passing day it appeared they had plenty. Brenda, too, had been left with half a house and had to reborrow to buy Harry out.

'And he didn't own that flat in London, either. That's in Miss Jones's name. So where did his money go? We need to look into that more closely.'

'Go on, what about the other one? Pat Walters?' Ian clarified. He got up to stretch his legs. He had spent most of the afternoon going over statements and the zilch information contained in the reports from the house-to-house teams.

'You saw her yourself, sir. It's hard to believe she's just lost a husband of almost nineteen years, she's more relieved than grieving. Anyway, the story's the same there. Even the daughter, Debbie, told me that although her father had been unhappy for a long time she knew he would never do anything to make anyone angry or upset.'

'There's no chance of it being an ex-patient or the relative of one, is there?'

Everyone groaned. The thought had passed through all their minds but to check back over almost a year of the comings and goings of everyone involved with Rickenham General was a daunting task, if not an impossible one. No one asked why this might be necessary. Patients and their relatives were at their most vulnerable in the rarified atmosphere of a hospital. And a couple of them in the room could remember a case where someone had

had it in for a hospital porter for some imagined mental cruelty. They were all thinking along the same lines – that the killer was one person – but this was dangerous when, in reality, there was nothing other than the scarves to suggest a connection. This was the recurring theme which ran through all their minds. The scarves had to mean something, but what?

Ian had already mentioned what Moira had said about both cases occurring out of doors.

'But one in the dark, one in daylight, sir,' Alan Campbell, as pedantic as ever had pointed out.

Another day was over with very little achieved, Ian thought as he draped his sheepskin over his arm and went downstairs. He was badly in need of a drink. This was another occasion when he would miss Barry Swan. They would have exchanged ideas as they relaxed over a couple of pints. Tonight he settled for his own company. Moira was out, going to the cinema with Deirdre. It was only days since the first murder and he hadn't been in on the start yet it seemed to have been with him for ever.

By this stage there were usually a couple of likely suspects, or at least a familiar quickening of the pulse when you knew someone was lying, but the friends and families of the deceased appeared to be beyond reproach as were the men themselves, discounting De Quincy's predilection for more than one girl-friend. So where did they look for that elusive factor, the motive? If you had a suspect you could look for the motive afterwards but this time they would have to do it the other way around. The post-mortems had revealed nothing other than the injuries which had been apparent at the scene. The men were reasonably healthy, neither of them was drunk or had taken any illegal substances. Both had eaten lunch but had not lived to eat dinner. It seemed a shame that they had had to undergo the indignity of having their bodies taken to pieces then put back together again when nothing had been gained by it.

Everyone who had known De Quincy or Walters had made some sort of statement. Hundreds, probably thousands of words, but not one which led them any closer to the killer.

Ian had made one more grasping-at-straws connection. One killing had taken place after three thirty, the other at six thirty-five. Did this mean anything? Were the murders committed by someone who worked until, say, three o'clock? Well, that really narrows it down, he thought. Except we're talking about a weekend. It did narrow it down if he was right. How many people worked over a weekend? And the timing suggested shift work. He made a mental list of possibilities: hospitals, homes for the elderly, social services, cinema staff, pub staff, chefs, hotel workers, telephonists, public transport workers. He stopped there. What was the point? But the first two? De Quincy had met his death outside St Luke's, Walters in the grounds of Rickenham General. That has to be it, there must be some relevance, he told himself as he pushed open the door of the Crown and was treated to the sight of the cheerful face of Bob Jones who was in full flow behind the bar, arms resting on his shrinking stomach as he regaled a customer with the latest piece of gossip. For medical reasons he had been put on a special diet. It had not, as Ian had feared, impaired his sense of humour.

By the time he was on his third pint of Adnams bitter and in convivial conversation, several things had happened. Because his bleeper was switched off he was unaware of them. Working when he was supposed to be on leave was one thing, overtime was an entirely different matter. And he had promised Moira he would take her out for the meal that she had turned down on Monday on account of the crowds. She and Deirdre had gone to the five fifteen showing of the film they were seeing: there would be plenty of time afterwards.

'Go on, have another. We don't see you in here much these days.' Bob Jones's eyes twinkled mischievously and Ian was enjoying himself. No, not quite that, he realised, but he was relaxing. With the bathroom now finished he felt he deserved a break.

'Do we ring the Chief?' Alan asked Brenda. Although they were of equal rank it did not appear that way. Alan nearly always deferred to his female colleague.

'Best not. Anyway, believe it or not, Short's still on the premises.'

'Inspector Short to you, my lovely.' They had not heard him enter the room. He slithered around the building taking people by surprise even when they were expecting him. 'Don't you think we can cope without the Chief? Come on, my girl, he's waiting in the interview room practically foaming at the mouth.'

Brenda bit her tongue, almost having said, 'Detective Constable to you, Baldy.' But Short meant no harm and he hadn't been serious in saying he expected her to refer to him formally. She was tired. It had been a late night with Andrew, one she had enjoyed thoroughly and would like to repeat. How slowly they were taking things, how easily their conversations flowed. Andrew had done no more than kiss her until last night, slow, gentle kisses which made her feel as though she was dissolving. And then, at the end of a lovely evening spent in a restaurant . . . Not now, she told herself as she put Andrew to the back of her mind, but she was still smiling as she followed Short along the corridor and downstairs, taking the cue from his purposeful but silent progress.

'Eric James Hudson. I do believe we've met before.' John Short gave him the benefit of his avuncular smile and pulled out a chair for Brenda, much to her astonishment, before he sat down himself.

'Yeah. I know,' Jimmy Hudson muttered sullenly when the proceedings had been explained to him and he had been asked if he understood them. The tape-recorder was now running.

Eric had always been known by his second name, and only then as Jimmy. He had a pathetic history of minor acts of violence. This chronicle reached way back into his childhood, causing him to have been excluded from school, where he had been labelled as a bully, on numerous occasions. For the evening of De Quincy's murder he had a perfect alibi, unless the Colchester police were lying.

Short toyed with his moustache. Only now did it strike him as odd that Hudson should have had such an alibi. He was known as a trouble-maker at Rickenham Athletic's ground, but only so far as away supporters were concerned. He would stand on the terraces and hurl verbal abuse at them. It was only afterwards, once they were well away from the ground and on their way home, that he would pick on a solitary away fan, one who was smaller than himself, and inflict some damage. Presumably, Short thought, he did not believe in shitting on his own doorstep. Or else he didn't want to be banned from the ground. Yet on the day of an important cup match for Rickenham he had gone to watch Colchester play. Had he known what was going to happen and steered clear of the action? Not only clear – at the relevant time he had been enjoying tea and sandwiches at the taxpayers' expense because he had taken it into his head to rearrange the features of someone who had jeered at his shirt, mistakenly taking the black and white stripes of the Rickenham strip for that of Newcastle United. The youth involved had been too thick to notice the thin red dividing line between the other two colours. But then, Jimmy had been even more stupid for flattening him in front of two policemen and several dozen witnesses. Hudson, Short thought in his clichéd way, has always been a farthing short of a penny. He'd missed Saturday's game and was about to miss this evening's. 'What've you got to say for yourself this time, lad?'

Brenda shuddered, wishing that the inspector would refrain from using dialogue from the era of *Dixon of Dock Green*.

'I was provoked. It was self-defence, ask anyone.'

'Certainly. If you just give me their names.' Rickenham Athletic had another home match that evening, a league match which had been rearranged because of their cup run. Hudson had been arrested before the game had begun and had now missed it. Kick-off was ten minutes ago.

Jimmy looked down at his hands which were clasped loosely and hung between his lumpy knees. He was clad in the uniform of his peer group: high tops, black nylon tracksuit bottoms which were too long and sported two white stripes down the sides, and a football shirt. But Short was unable to decipher the badge because it was hidden beneath a quilted jacket distinctly reminiscent of a Michelin Man. The sponsor's name, which was just visible between the jacket lapels, meant nothing to him either as football was anathema to Short.

Hudson remained silent.

'Look, son. The man you knifed had to be taken to casualty, and there's no question but that you put him there. This is by no means your first offence. You know what'll happen to you now, don't you? Why on earth do you do it? For God's sake, before the game, too.' Short shook his head in despair. Trying to put himself in Jimmy's place, he was sure he would have waited at least until he knew the result, but then, in Jimmy's head, the lift didn't stop at every floor.

'I was provoked,' he repeated.

Short looked at Brenda with despair. You try, his expression suggested. Jimmy knew his answers were being recorded, he was no stranger to police stations. With his second sentence he had admitted his guilt, and had done so again with his third.

'Why were you carrying a knife, Jimmy?' Brenda asked quietly. She understood that there was sufficient evidence for the Crown Prosecution to be completely satisfied that the case could go to trial. That was not the reason for this interview. Jimmy Hudson did not usually go armed, and that was very important.

'You got to these days. You never know what might happen at a match.'

'At Rickenham Athletic?' The worst trouble she could recall at the ground was when two fathers who had sons in the under-twelves side had come to blows. Yes, Eric James Hudson was a trouble-maker, but he had not gone to these lengths before. 'Cup match, was it, tonight?'

'Nah. League.'

'But you missed them winning in the last round of the cup?'

'I knew they'd do all right.'

Something wasn't quite right and both Brenda and John Short knew it. 'Why Colchester?' Brenda asked.

Jimmy Hudson shrugged. There was a sheen of sweat on his round, deceptively childlike face. 'Fancied a change, that's all. No law against it, is there? Anyway, they've done me for what happened there.'

'Yes. But it hasn't stopped you, has it? This time you went even further. You might have killed that man.'

'Come on, it was only his arm. He was taking the piss. No one understands. Rickenham's my team but I've got others as well. All they know is Manchester United and stuff like that.'

Brenda was puzzled. 'You wore a Rickenham shirt to Colchester and a Norwich one to Rickenham tonight?'

'Yeah. Always a different one from the match I'm watching.'

'I see.' He had his own peculiar logic, she supposed. It was Brenda who had realised that the shirt he was wearing was that of the Chief's team, Norwich City, the Canaries. And Hudson had been carrying a knife, one which he had not been afraid to use. There had to be some relevance here even if she couldn't see it. Someone had draped a Norwich City scarf around De Quincy's and Walters' necks and Walters had been stabbed. If DCI Roper had been present he would have recognised the shirt immediately.

'Jimmy, do you own a Norwich City scarf?'

He frowned, unsure where the question was leading. 'No. Never go in for scarves. Only the shirts. I've got eighteen different ones now. Except they keep changing them. They've even changed the Norwich colours. This is the old top. I'm keeping it, it's traditional,' he added with what might have been pride or simply determination that he wouldn't be rooked by the people who made a fortune out of selling replica kits.

All right, so they knew where he had been on Saturday evening, but where was he on Sunday afternoon Brenda asked him.

'At my mum's place. They let me go. I had to go back Monday, to the court.'

And no doubt Mrs Hudson would verify this even if she hadn't set eyes on her son for a month. We should have contacted the Chief, after all, Brenda realised belatedly. His knowledge of football was encyclopedic and his understanding of it would have gone a long way towards getting the truth out of Jimmy Hudson.

Having refused the services of a solicitor, he was charged and locked up for the night. 'Lawyers don't understand me no better than you,' he had told them earlier on. Brenda suspected he didn't even understand himself. But this time there would be more than money involved. On Monday Hudson had escaped with an order to pay damages and costs; he had only inflicted one blow upon his tormenter. The man he had put in Rickenham General was not in any danger, his flesh wound was apparently superficial, but by using a knife Jimmy Hudson had moved up a notch in the criminal hierarchy.

Having gone past the stage where nothing but bed was welcome, Brenda realised she was over-tired. She felt restless and unable to decide what to do with herself. Her jumping nerves were due to an excess of caffeine as well as a lack of sleep.

Inspector Short, for all his slobbish ways, appeared no different from when he had arrived that morning. 'Fancy a drink, love?' he asked now.

The 'love' grated but Brenda knew it was useless to say anything. To Short, all women were 'love'. Going back to her soulless, modern house, half-furnished, the legacy of her marriage to Harry, was the last thing which appealed. But soon it wouldn't matter. The woman at the mortgage broker's was ringing back at the end of the week. Soon she would own a home not a house.

Short decided to avoid the town centre pubs where they were likely to run into colleagues. The George was quiet enough but he thought it pretentious with its waistcoated barmen and an abundance of cherry plush and gilt-framed mirrors. The Crown would do and it wasn't far to walk.

The last Frampton bus was leaving its stop as they crossed the road. Only three passengers boarded it. There were few other people around despite the rise in temperature. Rickenham Green was like a ghost town, as if the residents had moved away *en masse* or else they were saving themselves for Christmas. When they reached the main bus-stops a few youths, aged no more than thirteen or fourteen, hung around, trying unsuccessfully to skateboard up and down the library steps. The sound of their clattering wheels echoed emptily.

'Where the hell is everybody?' Short muttered. There was not even much traffic.

When he veered down the alley that led between the High Street shops and the green, Brenda wondered if Short had an ulterior motive for choosing the Crown. Perhaps he was hoping to encounter the Chief.

As soon as they entered, Ian's tall figure could be seen at the bar, his back to them. It was also relatively quiet in the normally busy pub.

'Ah! Some comrades-in-arms,' Ian said by way of greeting, his sibilants none too crisp. 'What'll it be?'

Short and Brenda exchanged a grin. The Chief was not renowned for his alacrity in offering to buy a drink. Brenda asked for her usual, which was Campari and soda, no ice, Short for a pint of bitter. He caught sight of his reflection in the glass behind the bottles at the back of the bar and hastily flipped some strands of hair back into place. They had been resting on his shoulder exposing the partial baldness he hated so much. It was his only vanity.

Ian's face was flushed; it did not seem an appropriate time to start discussing cases, but Brenda found herself unable to resist. They took their drinks to a table in a corner.

'Can we have been right?' Ian asked upon hearing the news of Hudson's arrest. 'Is this, in the end, all about football?' He spoke to the room in general as he was finding difficulty in focusing upon the faces of the two people nearest him. 'We'd better check.'

There were lists of known football trouble-makers along with plenty of video footage. But would the names and faces of these people be any use here? Neither of the victims were football supporters and, Ian realised, there was nothing to connect De Quincy to football at all. 'Mrs Smith,' he enunciated carefully, aware of the dangers of the letter S when Adnams bitter was involved, 'do you think she was making it all up? Did she, in fact, see anything at all? Or, if she did, has she distorted it? Man A comes down the road. No scarf. Man B follows, wearing a scarf. But supposing Man A was actually Man B?'

'Sir?' Brenda wondered just how long Ian had been in the Crown.

'I think what Sir is trying to say,' Short interrupted with a touch of sarcasm, 'is that De Quincy might have been the second man, might, for all we know, have set upon the first man and got himself killed for his efforts. Mrs Smith's initial statement is now open to question.'

'Quite,' Ian commented, having decided the fewer words the better. 'A Canaries scarf.' He cursed for not being able to think coherently. 'Dammit. It must be relevant. Talk to the man who was attacked tonight. Find out if he's local or if he was with the opposition. Find out who he supports and why Hudson went to such extremes. Okay, he was safely out of the way on Saturday, too safely, perhaps, but if he's that fanatical who knows what he may have set up. Because if, by any chance, De Quincy *was* wearing a Norwich scarf ... well, I think you know what I'm getting at.'

They did. Locals should support Rickenham Athletic and Ipswich. At least, that's how they read Ian's reasoning. He was an exception but that, as in most things, was par for the course.

'If Hudson is involved it would make the cases independent of each other,' Brenda said. 'He can't possibly have killed De Quincy.'

A thoughtful silence followed this comment until Short offered to buy another round.

Ian eyed his glass. 'Just a half for me, thanks,' he said. 'You might think it ridiculous, Brenda, but somehow I feel there's something personal here,' he continued when Short went to the bar. 'Believe me, it isn't the drink talking. Anyway, see what you can turn up on known offenders. Ah, thanks, John.' Ian took a sip from his glass. 'Look into the ringleaders especially.'

Brenda nodded. She knew what was going through his mind. The hooligans inflicted the damage but the men who orchestrated the attacks were often in good jobs and drove expensive cars. Aged between the early twenties and the late thirties they seemed to get their kicks that way; in the organisation of violence rather than the participation. And De Quincy fitted the bill as an organiser. Anne Morrisson had admitted he lived for excitement. The motive for his killing might be revenge.

But they were thinking in circles. John Short levered his body out of the chair and made his way to the Gents, stopping on the way back to ring the station. Whoever was covering nights might just as well make themselves useful by getting a list of local names ready for the morning. There wouldn't be many, the really nasty specimens came from the cities. But the Chief was right, it was worth a try. Anything was at this stage.

He returned to the table. 'One of the big houses in Saxborough Road's been done,' he said, screwing up his face as Brenda put the slice of lemon from her drink into her mouth and began to chew. He loosened his tie and undid the top button of his shirt. They were almost on top of the log fire and it was throwing out a lot of heat. Short rather liked the place with its low, beamed ceilings – original, he knew, not some awful conversion – and its flagstoned floor. 'In and away. Plenty of fingerprints round the place, though, so we might strike lucky.'

'Anyone we know?' Brenda asked, having finished chewing.

'A Mrs Fletcher. Barbara, I think they said her name was. Lives alone. Must rattle round like a pea in a can in that place. Know her?'

Neither Ian nor Brenda did. They shook their heads.

'Anyway, Danny Cotton seems to be the flavour of the month there. She told the patrol team who responded to her call that he's wonderful, can't do enough for her, advised her about security and so on. All I can say is that he can't have done much of a job if someone got in so easily.'

Danny Cotton. Ian thought hard. Yes, a PC who, whilst capable enough, was inclined to be lazy. On the other hand he was very good with the general public and had been given the job as a community officer on the basis that, hopefully, that was where his talents lay. A couple of pints hasn't impaired the old memory, he congratulated himself. A couple? More like six. He must go after this last half or Moira would be furious. 'Was much taken?'

'In size, no. In value, yes.'

'How much?' Ian took an interest in all crimes committed within their division even if he was not directly involved. Nothing worked in isolation, including criminals. There were always links to be found. Ian sighed. This time it sounded as if the thief had been clever but he did not know any clever criminals. Then he smiled. Of course he didn't. It was the clever ones they failed to catch. 'What did he get?'

Short grunted. 'Cash. Couple of hundred quid left lying about in the kitchen. Several rings, likewise, although Mrs Fletcher apparently owns enough to adorn her toes and fingers twice over. The rest were upstairs. Couple of small bits of silver and a porcelain ornament. Over ten grand's worth in a minute or two and no trouble getting in or out. He'd legged it before anyone had a chance to call us.'

'Burglar alarm?'

'Yes. But the neighbours were either out or ignored it. You know how it is. Anyway, our man covered a pane of glass in sticky stuff before smashing it then reached in and unbolted the back door at the top.'

'I thought you said Cotton had checked it out.'

'He did. But the thief reached in through the cat-flap and managed to undo the bottom lock as well.'

'I really must go. I'm supposed to be taking Moira out.' Ian stood, steadying his chair as he did so. The front legs clattered back down on the flagstones. 'See you tomorrow.'

Brenda and Short watched his progress towards the door, both grimacing as he approached a low beam. It was long practice which caused him to duck rather than returning sobriety.

'He's pissed,' Short said without ceremony then downed his own drink. 'Want another?'

'I might as well.' Brenda tried not to picture Moira Roper's evening.

Richie Andrews was not at home when DS Markham rang his bell at nine thirty on Wednesday evening. Not at home – or not answering the door. He tried again, leaving his finger on the bell longer than was necessary, then he gave up, turned his back and walked down the steps to the street.

The moon was almost full and gave the night sky a strange quality as it competed with the glow of the sodium lamps. Markham crossed the road, turned to face the converted house and saw that no lights shone from the front window of Andrews' flat. It was then that he noticed the sky. There were no stars. Cloud cover obscured them but left a gap as though to frame the moon. As he watched a thin greyness, like a bride's veil, drifted across the surface of the moon. Markham, who did not know the meaning of the word 'metaphor', recognised that this was what might be happening to them. The solution to the murders was eluding them because they were seeing things in a distorted way; they were missing some essential ingredient because they were not looking beyond the curtain, only at it. And in much the same way there was something bothering him, something he knew he ought to remember, but it, too, eluded him. Julie was too much on his mind again. Thoughts of her weakened him.

Markham stated walking, heading nowhere in particular. He was frustrated. Even he had been following the rules, more or less, but two men were dead and no one knew why.

As he retraced his steps he noticed there were now more pedestrians in the High Street. The cinema, reopened after standing derelict for years, now housed three screens and was well attended. Its brightly lit façade stood out over the dimmer lights of the shops. The take-away places were busy. Judging by the amount of food that was dropped or thrown away in disgust, Markham wondered why anyone patronised them in the first place.

Where would someone like Richie Andrews be on a night like this? Markham could not begin to guess. Maybe he was at home after all, in bed with some girl. He decided to try once more then leave it until another time, not at all certain now why he had decided he wanted to see him.

His mouth stretched in a cynical grin when, heading towards him from the opposite end of Saxborough Road, he saw the man in question. Automatically he checked his watch. It was quarter-past ten. The two men's footsteps took them to the steps leading up to Richie's house simultaneously.

Richie frowned in what Markham took to be non-recognition when he introduced himself.

'We've met before. Obviously you don't remember. I called around earlier. I just happened to be passing. How're you doing?' Small talk was not Markham's forte and he knew he sounded stilted. At least he had come up with a reasonable excuse to be speaking to him at all.

'Fine. Look, I'm knackered.' Richie paused, then smiled widely, showing good teeth in a generous mouth. Even in the semi-darkness he appeared feverish. 'If you want to chat, why don't you come up?'

The invitation was totally unexpected. Markham took a second to reply. 'Thanks. I will.'

The front door was surprisingly secure. He followed Richie into the large hallway which had been designed with room for a table and two chairs and a large Victorian pram. It had not been tampered with. A graceful staircase rose from the centre and doorways led off from the black and white ceramic tiles. It was all much better than Markham had expected. At the top of the stairs the polished boards could be seen on either side of a runner which continued down the length of the landing. It was here that Richie stopped to unlock his own door. Richie's flat was not a disappointment after the downstairs grandeur. There was a small vestibule with doors leading off. The main room, into which he was shown, had not been altered either and retained its original proportions. It was large with an elaborate ceiling rose and matching cornice. The soft furnishings were elegant and in muted shades, the dining-table was chrome and glass. It was many steps up from the usual Saxborough Road flats. What was missing was a lack of identity. There were no personal items, all the surfaces were bare as though Richie meant his stay there to be short. The only surprising touch was the pile of newspapers in the corner. They were, Markham saw, editions of the *Rickenham Herald*. It seemed that Richie took an interest in local matters.

'I've got some beer,' Richie said. 'Have a seat and I'll get it.' He returned from the kitchen with several cans and a couple of glasses which he placed on the table. 'Help yourself.'

Markham got up and did so. He pulled the ring-tab off with a hiss of escaping gas whilst he watched Richie cross the room and remove his overcoat. Then he disappeared for a minute or so. He's excited about something, Markham thought. He almost looks ill. There were two patches of colour in his cheeks and his eyes shone unnaturally brightly. When he returned, minus the coat, his hand shook minimally as he lifted his beer to his lips and tilted his head back to swallow.

His willingness to entertain Markham was puzzling. The sergeant had expected to hold a brief conversation in the street from which he would leave with his questions unanswered. But now he had the opportunity to do so there were no questions he could think of to ask, except one, and that was how did he cope? It would be better to wait and see what developed.

'You said you were passing. Something in particular you wanted to see me about?' There was a sly expression on Richie's face, an almost mocking grin on his lips. He was struggling not to laugh.

Markham chose his words with care. 'I may have been wrong about you. I imagined that we'd have met again before now.'

'No. I learned my lesson, as they say. Straight as a die now, as they also say.' He turned away, feeling the internal laughter pulling at his mouth.

'Glad to hear it. It's almost a year now since Martin died, I just thought I'd see how you're doing.'

Since Martin died. The words chilled him and the hatred nearly rose to the surface. Martin didn't die, he was as good as murdered, he wanted to scream. 'Yes, well, it hasn't been easy. All I'd ever known was him and me.' Talk normally, he thought, don't let the bastard know how you're feeling, kid him on a bit more. 'It took a while, but I'm just starting to get over it. He was more than a friend to me.' Richie stopped. If he carried on he'd become maudlin and there was no way he was going to allow Markham to witness his anguish.

'Are you working?'

Richie took a long swallow of his drink. 'I'm in between jobs at the moment,' he lied. 'You know how it is. And there's my allowance.' He held out his hands in mock despair. 'No qualifications, you see. Plenty of brains but nothing to show for them.'

Markham wondered what exactly was going through Richie's mind. He had blamed the police for Martin's death, but Martin had been caught committing a crime and the pursuit car had been travelling within the speed limit, following rather than chasing. Martin had been the one driving dangerously fast. It had cost him his life.

'Want another one?' Richie indicated the cans of beer.

'No, thanks. I can't stay. See you around.' Markham let himself out and ran down the stairs and into the street, aware that he was being watched from the upstairs window where the curtains were still undrawn.

But he probably wouldn't see him around. Whatever else he might have been lying about, Richie, like his friend Martin, was not known to frequent pubs.

Markham began to make his way home. Tomorrow he'd have a word with Danny Cotton and ask him to keep an eye on Richie. Tonight he would be lazy and settle for a pizza and then he would sit down and think, try to recall what it was that had prompted him to speak to Richie Andrews.

But the pizza congealed in the box and Markham, for once out of control, drank half a bottle of Scotch. He knew too much drink was the cause of his tears and he brushed them away with the back of his hand. Nine years yet he could not forget her. Moving away from Nottingham had achieved nothing. Why should he have expected it to when Julie was with him wherever he went? They had been together since their last year in school. He had never wanted another woman. And then she had developed leukaemia. For the next six years he had watched her die. But she wouldn't marry him, not once she knew. She said she wanted to leave him free for someone else. How could there be anyone else? And what had she meant by free? They had been living together, as good as married, for years.

And that was the reason for his fascination with Richie Andrews, he realised. From the time of the accident he had known that Cooper was to Andrews what Julie had been to him, that both he and Andrews had no need of other people except for the ones they had lost. And Markham knew how the hatred had grown inside him with nothing at which to direct it, how he wanted to lash out at everyone and everything. But he had kept a tight control and still did so, although it had become easier with practice.

So how does he cope? he wanted to know.

The tears had stopped. Markham picked up the bottle and refilled his glass. Just once in a while he allowed himself an indulgence. And tonight he needed it.

The laughter could no longer be contained. Richie was bent double, tears rolling down his face. Each time he tried to control it it welled up again until his sides ached and he was breathless. He knew he was on the verge of hysteria. What a fool Markham was, what an absolute bloody fool. He had stood within feet of him, near enough to touch him and what his coat pockets had contained. Of course Richie had recognised Markham, how would he ever be able to forget his face? Seeing him approach had given him a fright until he realised that if he was about to be arrested Markham would not have come alone.

And what about that copper, Danny Cotton? Cotton seemed to have no idea who Richie was but he was up to something. He had seen him enter 101 Saxborough Road more than once. It might be useful to find out his connection with the occupier of that house.

The laughter subsided. Another two weeks until Christmas then ten days after that took him to the anniversary of Martin's death. But before that he had to endure his first Christmas alone. Martin had always seen to things, had always ensured they had the best of everything.

His eyes grew brighter. Bile filled his throat as his hatred threatened to choke him. He had been living on his nerves for too long. His obsession had taken over his life. He felt a silent scream deep within him but only a groan escaped his lips. Never in his life had he felt so determined to go through with anything, and he would do so without conscience and without caring if he got caught. He had nothing left to lose.

<h1 style="text-align:center">7</h1>

What now? Ian wondered. He sighed with resignation as he said, 'I think we'd better have a word, then. Get him in as soon as possible.'

It had been brought to the attention of one of the officers dealing with the burglary in Saxborough Road that, of the five most common sets of prints found in Barbara Fletcher's house, one was, naturally, her own, a second was that of her cleaner and a third belonged to PC Danny Cotton. Mrs Fletcher could not say with any certainty who may have left the other prints. 'I entertain quite a lot, and it's usually the same small crowd. Bridge, drinks, that sort of thing.' The lifted prints had been matched against those of known criminals and, because she had mentioned PC Cotton and his visits, against his too, simply to rule them out so they could concentrate on the others.

'But everywhere?' Markham had queried when he passed the information on to Ian. 'And most of them in the lounge and one of the bedrooms.'

Police corruption was by no mean unheard of and anything even slightly untoward needed immediate investigation.

Ian, vaguely hung-over, could not bear the thought of another of their kind being bent. But it was known that Danny had three children and another one on the way. It was also known that he was amiable and pleasant-looking and would have found no difficulty in talking his way into people's homes.

Nothing like being invited in to case the joint, Ian thought cynically. It felt as though everyone and everything was against him at the moment. Last night his wife had backed away as he had stooped to kiss her. 'You reek of beer,' she had told him, wrinkling her nose. 'How many have you had?' When he told her she had said that going out was not such a good idea after all. They had ended up with a Chinese take-away eaten in silence.

And now, on top of two murders, there was the possibility that PC Cotton had wandered from the primrose path. 'Oh, Christ!'

Alan Campbell's head jerked up. Blasphemy was against everything his puritanical upbringing had taught him.

Ian was shaking his head. Being around Inspector Short for too long had induced him to start thinking in clichés. Ian hated clichés, but he knew himself well enough to realise that there were more things in the modern world he hated than liked, and that he was banging his head against a brick wall wishing things were otherwise. And before he could curse at that second, unbidden cliché Danny Cotton tapped on the door.

'Let's go upstairs,' Ian said. 'Alan?'

Alan put down whatever he was reading with reluctance. He had had an idea. It was vague in its form and he wanted to think about it.

Danny Cotton was sandwiched between the tall solid figure of the chief inspector and the thin, weaselly Scotsman. As an intimidating tactic it was good. Chance alone had put Danny in such a position but he did not know that. His hands were damp and he felt the sweat soaking into his shirt beneath his jacket. He was about to become unemployed because of what he'd done and because he'd withheld information and Jackie would leave him because of his infidelity and, deep down, he knew he deserved it.

It was to Ian's office on the top floor of the building to which he was taken. They walked the length of the corridor to the sound of clacking word processor keys. Here the secretaries were housed. It was usually the quietest part of the building.

Ian inclined his head towards a chair and Danny sat down with an air of discomfort. No one enjoyed being hauled upstairs. Ian hoped this was the reason for his shiftiness rather than guilt. 'You know Barbara Fletcher, I believe?'

He swallowed hard. This was it, then. 'Yes, sir. She lives on my patch.'

'How well do you know her?' Ian took his own seat behind the desk. Alan sat to one side of Cotton.

Danny felt the heat rise from somewhere around his collar bone. More sweat broke out on his forehead. At least he could answer truthfully. 'I stop for a chat sometimes. She showed me over the house once when we were discussing security. She lives on her own, you see, and it's a big place. I warned her to be careful.'

'Showed you around once?'

'Yes, sir. That was all that was necessary.'

He was lying and they knew it. There was no way he could have left so many clear sets of prints upstairs on a single visit. Ian changed tack. 'Has DS Markham spoken to you recently?'

'Yes. About Richie Andrews. He asked me to keep an eye on his movements.'

'Do you know Andrews?'

'No, sir.'

So Cotton was proving to be a failure as a community officer, too. His first priority should have been to acquaint himself with the villains and suspected villains before ingratiating himself with the likes of Mrs Fletcher. Not that Andrews fitted into that category, he had form but had not been in trouble since that one occasion. 'Then get to know him. And quickly.' I bet he knows you, Ian thought. 'What size shoes do you take?'

Danny was confused. The whole day had been confusing. He had been asked to return to the station mid-shift because the Chief wanted a word with him. Now he was asking about his shoe size. 'Tens, sir.'

Tens. Ian glanced down at his feet. Yes, they looked big enough for tens. Not Danny's footprints inside the back door on the kitchen floor, then. They had been a size eight, the imprint, where it was clear, that of a pair of almost smooth-soled shoes. Not trainers – that in itself was unusual nowadays.

'Tell me, Constable Cotton, what is it exactly that you do upstairs in Mrs Fletcher's house?' Ian asked conversationally.

Alan Campbell was not participating in the interview, he was merely there as a witness. But he felt a tremor of pity for the man sitting rigidly in his seat, unable to speak.

'Nothing,' Danny finally said with a catch in his throat.

'Last night her house was broken into.' Ian noted the look of shock on his face. 'Valuables and cash were taken.'

'And you think I did it?' Danny sat bolt upright, his incredulity genuine. But Ian also noted the relief flood into his face.

'Did you?'

'I did not, sir.'

'Then you have nothing to worry about.'

Thinking he was about to be dismissed, Danny relaxed, but he shrank back in his chair when DCI Roper asked how his family was. 'They're fine, thank you. Except Jackie gets tired a lot at the moment.'

'That's understandable.' Cotton's fingerprints had been most numerous in the lounge and one of the bedrooms. The most likely explanation was that he was having a fling with Barbara Fletcher. She lived alone, she was possibly lonely and she was said to be good-looking. With three children, another on the way and a wife who was constantly tired, an older, glamorous female might seem like a tempting alternative to the domesticity of his present home life.

There was little Ian could do about it unless these activities were taking place whilst Cotton was on duty. 'Good,' he said. 'Many people would envy you. You have a happy, healthy young family. Don't do anything to jeopardise what you have.'

'No, sir. I won't.'

But the way in which Danny lowered his eyes as he spoke told Ian all he wanted to know. His assumption was correct. And Cotton was scared; the warning may well be enough to put an end to it. 'You can go now.'

Danny got up stiffly. His legs felt weak as though he had been partaking in strenuous exercise. He ran a hand through his spiky black hair and swallowed. 'Thank you.'

Ian and Alan watched him leave. 'Why do they do it?' Ian asked rhetorically before remembering that Alan had divorced because his marriage was a sham. His wife had been appearing in hard core pornography, a fact which had come to light during a criminal investigation.

The phone rang. There was a woman waiting to see him downstairs, he was informed. 'Her name's Miss Charlotte Jones.'

It took Ian a second to realise who she was. Something important must have occurred to have brought her up from London. He told Alan he wasn't needed and waited for Miss Jones to be shown up. Miss, not Ms, he noted with satisfaction.

She's stunning, was Ian's initial reaction before he realised it was only the impression she gave. There was something about the way in which she held herself, some sort of inner confidence and belief in herself which shone through. And she was clearly furious. Her figure was slender and nicely proportioned but, on closer inspection, her face was all wrong. Or should have been. The nose was a little too sharp, the grey eyes a little too wide apart and the generous mouth above the firm chin reminded Ian of the endless stream of blonde actresses with too perfect teeth which America seemed to produce. The dark brown hair had a natural curl and was cut, wedge-like, at ear level. It really suited her. He guessed that her complexion was normally paler than at that moment as she stood in the doorway flushed with anger. 'Please come in and sit down, Miss Jones,' he said courteously.

'Thank you.' The two clipped words showed the difficulty she had in controlling her feelings.

Ian waited, his forearms resting easily on the blotter on his desk. She needed a second or two to frame her thoughts into words.

'I want to know everything. I want to know who this woman is who stole Justin from me. And I want to know why he was killed. She's involved, she has to be. It happened here, didn't it?'

This unexpected visit was not, after all, important. It was no more than the curiosity of one woman needing to find out about the usurper of her man's affections. He wondered why females had this obsession to check out the opposition, to make comparisons, favourable or otherwise, to try to discover what it was that the other possessed which made them more attractive to a man. It was, like anything to do with female psychology, impenetrable to Ian. 'Miss Jones, I can understand what a shock you've had and how upsetting all this has been but I'll be blunt with you. Justin was already living with Miss Morrisson before he met you.'

'I don't believe you.' She tugged at the hem of her short, black skirt. A three-quarter length mustard coat had fallen open to reveal a boat-neck lambswool sweater, also in black.

'I'm not in the habit of lying,' Ian answered quietly. 'At the moment we know how Justin died and when, but we don't know why.'

'In other words you've no idea who killed him. Could she have done it?'

The wide apart eyes met Ian's. 'No,' he said, knowing to whom she was referring.

'Are you sure?'

'Yes.' It felt as if he was being interrogated but he sensed some inner turmoil was responsible. Charlotte Jones was holding something back.

'There aren't . . .' she paused 'They're aren't any children, are there?'

'No.'

The tension drained away, leaving her face and posture more relaxed. 'Thank God for that,' she whispered. Her hand, without her seeming to realise it, came to rest on her stomach.

She's pregnant, Ian thought. Had De Quincy known? If so, and Charlotte had intended giving up work and her weekend visits to her parents, how would he have coped? What possible excuse could he have found for disappearing every weekend? 'Miss Jones?'

She was staring into space and there were tears in her eyes. She sniffed once and looked him in the face. 'I'm having his baby.'

'Did you mention this to the police when they spoke to you?' This visit was important after all. The baby put a whole new perspective on the case. It was a complication De Quincy surely could not have welcomed.

'No. It didn't seem relevant. I mean, at the time I didn't know about the other woman. Then when they came back and told me he had been living a double life I could have killed him myself.'

'Did Justin know about the baby?'

'Yes.'

'Was he pleased?'

She shrugged and her coat came further apart showing full breasts and a flat stomach. 'You know how men are. My friends who've had children tell me they're often ambiguous until the baby's born. Afraid of the loss of freedom and the extra financial dependence whilst at the same time smirking with pride that they're going to be a father.'

It appeared that Miss Jones's awareness of the psychology of the opposite sex was far greater than his. 'What were your plans, for after the birth?'

'I hadn't made any. I wasn't sure whether I'd want to go back to work and leave him with anyone.'

Him? Charlotte Jones was further advanced in her pregnancy

than he would have guessed if she was at the stage where the sex of the child had been revealed to her. Justin might have had time to make contingency plans. 'How did Justin feel about that?'

'He said the choice was mine, to wait and see how I felt. But he did say it would mean it would be some time before he could pay me back, so I got the impression he'd prefer I went back to work as soon as possible.'

'Pay you back?'

'Yes. I lent him some money.'

'May I ask what for?' Surely the Met had checked on his financial position. But this was a private loan, between lovers. There would have been no reason for Charlotte to have mentioned it unless she was specifically asked.

She sighed deeply and folded her hands in her lap. Ian saw how much courage it took for her to admit to the humiliation she had suffered.

'He told me that his parents lived here in Rickenham Green. It was something I believed we had in common – only children of elderly parents. He said his mother needed one of those chair-lift things for the stairs and other alterations to the house because she was becoming more and more disabled. My parents are in much the same position, and they've always said they never want to leave their home. They can afford to stay there, though.

'My flat is expensive. I was keeping my head above water but I insisted Justin share the costs when he moved in and he did so. I really believed he loved me, you see. We'd each got our own lifestyle and friends and we spent most weekends apart, but what we had during the week was perfect. Well, I thought it was perfect. When he said he needed the money and what it was for I didn't hesitate in lending it to him.'

'Miss Jones, excuse me, but just now you said that you were keeping your head above water. How were you able to find the money?'

'I withdrew it from my building society account. It was a sum my parents had given me when I moved to London but it was on the condition it was only to be used in an emergency. I'd kept to my word and I was determined to manage by myself.'

'I don't wish to embarrass you, but I need to know – '

'How much?' she interrupted. There was a tight smile on her lips. 'Ten thousand pounds.'

Ten thousand pounds out of pocket, no one now to help pay the mortgage and a child on the way. On top of all that, the man whom she loved, and who she believed loved her, had been living with another woman and was now dead. Ian had also added to her misery by telling her that Justin had known Anne before Charlotte came on the scene. And I thought the world was against me, Ian thought. 'Now you've had time to consider it, have you any idea what he really needed the money for?' De Quincy's parents lived abroad. They had been informed and were coming back for the funeral, whenever that might take place, but they had not been a close family. He could not begin to guess how this funeral would be arranged, not with the two women involved. But there could be no burial yet. If – when, he added optimistically – they arrested a suspect who then denied his guilt the defence lawyers might well demand a second post-mortem.

'For her. That's what makes me so sick. How could he have taken my money and given it to another woman? My God, I believed every one of his lies.' She bit her lip, angry again. 'I want to see her.'

'You said it was a loan. He intended paying you back,' Ian said in an attempt to defuse her anger.

'Yes. But that was a year ago and he hadn't offered me any repayment. I assumed I'd get it in instalments.' She met his eyes. 'I expect you think I ought to have told the police about this, too. It didn't cross my mind, and at the time I really did think it was for his parents.'

'I can't imagine it would do any good for you to meet Miss Morrisson. However, I can't stop you, but I promise I'll go and see her myself and find out if anything can be done about the money. Have you any proof of the loan?'

Charlotte reached into her handbag and pulled out a crumpled piece of paper. She handed it to Ian. It contained a few lines written in, presumably, Charlotte's hand and undersigned by De Quincy. 'It isn't a legal document, but I did get him to sign that.'

Ian nodded. There would be no harm in asking Anne Morrisson firstly if she knew about the money and, secondly, what had happened to it if she did. Only then did it occur to him how little involvement he had had with the individuals in both these cases. At his rank there was not usually much direct contact, but Ian did not work that way; he liked to make a point of speaking to everyone concerned. So far, apart from Charlotte Jones, he had only met Pat Walters and her daughter. And now he was faced with two new facts. De Quincy had been about to become a father, and he owed money. 'Is there anything else you feel I ought to know?'

Charlotte shook her head and the dark curls rippled. 'You're right,' she said with a genuine smile. 'It wouldn't do any good going to see her. I should hate her on sight whatever she was like.' It was obvious there was something she wanted to say. Ian waited again. With bowed head she asked, 'Is she prettier than me?'

'No. She isn't,' he said emphatically, but hypocritically. He had just told her that he did not lie. However, it was unlikely that Anne Morrisson was quite as stunning and it had been worth it to see the pleasure in Charlotte's face, especially as it was likely to be the only bit of comfort she could hold on to during the coming months.

'Thank you.' She stood and buttoned her coat.

'How did you get here?'

'On the train. I don't have a car in London.'

'Then I'll arrange for someone to drive you to the station.' It had begun to rain. Ian had been conscious of the steady hiss although his back had been to the window. Now he turned to look. It was proper rain, unlaced with snow or sleet.

'You're very kind.'

He led her downstairs and watched her push through the revolving glass doors. Charlotte Jones would now have to rethink her whole life.

Ian told Short that if he was wanted he would be with Anne Morrisson. The sphere of the investigation was widening, including past friends and acquaintances of the murdered men. As the days went by it seemed more certain that one person had committed both crimes. One killer might get away with it, but surely not two in the same town. The dates, did they have any relevance? It was, Ian thought, something else to check, another fact to add to the files.

Alan Campbell stopped him on his way out. 'You wanted to know, sir,' Alan began defensively. 'The shoes. The burglary?' he added, recognising incomprehension in the Chief's face.

Ian rubbed his jaw between thumb and forefinger, feeling the prickle of bristles. Campbell's cheeks were as smooth as when he had arrived that morning. He shrugged his arms into his raincoat which he removed from a hook in the wall. The corridor had a peculiar odour reminiscent of wet uniforms. 'Yes, the shoes.' He had remembered.

'Forensics say they can't get a make but they think they might be hand-made.'

A burglar in hand-made shoes? Crime certainly does pay, Ian thought. 'And what do you make of that?'

Alan chewed his thin, colourless lips and considered the question before answering it. 'Search me,' was the best he could come up with.

'If you ask me, I think it's taking the piss.'

'Yes, sir.' Alan went back to the room from which he had come. He was never sure how to take the Chief's moods.

Anne Morrisson was alone when Ian arrived unannounced. Her sister, she told him, had gone to the supermarket, which stayed open late on Thursdays and Fridays. 'There wasn't much in and I thought I ought to eat,' she said in a way which suggested she felt ashamed that her body was functioning at all. Ian suspected she would have eaten little during the days which had elasped since De Quincy's death.

Meeting Anne for the first time, Ian realised that, unwittingly, he had not lied to Charlotte Jones. Anne's figure was less clearly defined and there was a roundness about her which might later turn to fat. She was attractive but not glamorous and her hair was so pale it was almost white. Two opposites to look at, but they had in common the love and the loss of the same man.

The sister returned just as Ian was leaving. She was, as Brenda had said, capable and brisk and was not making the mistake of talking in whispers or treating Anne in any way differently from normal.

As he drove back to the station he thought about what Anne had told him and wondered what they could do about it.

He was a con man, Ian thought. He was more or less living off two women and deceiving them both at the same time. And now this. He patted the breast pocket of his jacket. He would drop the envelope containing the account and the cheque in at the station then go home and spend a quiet evening with his wife.

It was not to be. Not only had De Quincy picked up a hefty sum from some risky spread betting, but the City firm for whom he had worked had, whilst going through his client list, come across De Quincy's own portfolio. He was worth almost a million pounds.

So why had he borrowed ten thousand from Miss Jones? It wasn't a loan, Ian decided. The man had had no intention of paying it back. He had played both sides against the middle for long enough and, with the knowledge of the forthcoming baby, he knew he had to get out. He had been feathering his nest in order to be able to leave it.

Disgusted with himself for the mixture of inaccurate metaphor and cliché, he rang Moira to say he would be late then cursed Short to hell and back because the way in which he spoke seemed to be contagious.

Danny Cotton was still sweating when he went to bed that night. He had been so sure they knew, but he had been wrong. The Chief may have guessed that there was another woman, but not that it was Emma. And it was obvious now that they hadn't found out about De Quincy's sporadic visits to Barbara Fletcher's house. How pale Emma had been when she learned the name of the first victim. What must it have felt like to have slept with a murdered man? That she had, Danny was in no doubt. Danny had seen him at the house and recognised him when his photograph had been circulated. Now he was in deeper than ever. But the man had deserved to die, anyone who slept with Emma deserved to die.

He reached out for Jackie, suddenly grateful for her presence, but she pulled away, turning her back on him. Danny felt like crying.

8

Barbara Fletcher was shaken when she returned home from her Wednesday night bridge game to find the burglar alarm ringing unheeded. Letting herself in through the front door, she sensed that the house was now empty. The kitchen, humming with the quiet sounds of domestic appliances, became sharply bright and shadowless the instant she threw the light switch. There were footprints on the floor along with some shards of glass but most of the pane in the back door was still held in place by brown sticky tape. Within minutes she had assessed what had been taken and called the police. It was the intrusion which upset her more than the missing items. Yet this intrusion was not as bad as the one which had occurred about a year ago. She was still recovering from the shock of that. That the two events might be connected she did not realise until several days later but without jeopardising everything she had worked so hard for there was nothing she could do about it.

Once the police had left she picked up the telephone again. 'Emma, I'm glad I caught you. I think it's better if we cancel tomorrow evening. I've been burgled and I really can't face it.'

'How awful. Was much taken?'

'Enough. I hope you don't mind.' Barbara was aware that both girls were avaricious – combined with their looks it was what had led her to pick them. 'Would you do me a favour and let Molly know?'

'Of course I will. And, no, I don't mind. I could do with a night in.'

Barbara hung up. Emma had sounded relieved, which was worrying. She hoped she wasn't getting in too deeply with Danny Cotton because that would ruin everything.

The following morning she rang her clients at their respective places of work, explaining why it was inconvenient for them to come. Having done all this her mind returned to the burglary. Was it someone she knew, someone who had spotted the vulnerable point in her security? Enough people came and went. The irony was that she didn't have a cat. The previous owners had had the flap fitted. Could it be Danny, who had looked over the house in order to advise her and who had spent many hours under her roof since? She was aware of his involvement with Emma and his eternal lack of money, but would he repay her hospitality in that way? It was possible if he knew which items were of value and he wanted to set up home with Emma. On the other hand she doubted he would be that stupid. But then, would any of her clients? It was more likely an opportunist thief who had grabbed items at random. That was the most likely explanation.

Her life had almost turned full circle. From a distance those early days as a call girl seemed to belong to somebody else, but she would always be grateful to Michael Hammond. Michael had treated her well and sometimes took her out to dinner because she was beautiful and knew how to behave; through him she had met the man who was to become her husband. And Michael had been gentleman enough not to drop the slightest hint concerning her background. But once married she lacked excitement, and her older, albeit rich, husband seemed stolid and dull and the child a mere hindrance.

She stared at her face in the mirror which also reflected the cruel winter daylight. Not bad, she thought, smiling at her modesty.

But never again would she earn a living on her back. She had taken a more than generous settlement in return for her promise not to have anything more to do with her husband. And with it, almost to spite him because it would have offended his sensibilities so much, she employed her own girls.

But what if Emma moved in with Danny and it turned out he was really a thief? It was a stalemate. If she reported her suspicions she knew what he could do to her. And he would do it, she thought, because, if he was guilty of the robbery, he had nothing to lose. If he was innocent he would find a way of getting revenge. And who would believe her if she said he had made full use of her services? Emma would lie for him, of that she was certain. It had been her plan to have the local constable firmly under her control but things had got out of hand.

Leave things be, she decided, as she smoothed her hair into

place. It was a rule she had adhered to over the years. Leave well alone, don't look for trouble, might have been her motto. Without the girls she would have to sell up and buy somewhere smaller and although she would have an adequate income she did not want to have to do without the luxuries to which she had become accustomed. And she was too old to start again. Another couple of years, she reckoned, and then she could give it up and move away. With a fresh start she could become the person everyone thought her to be.

She was still shaking when she went to bed and had no idea how she had managed to remain calm in the presence of the police. She had hesitated before reporting the burglary until she realised that her insurance company would not pay out without a police reference number. Her worries had been groundless; the police had taken her call at face value, no questions had been asked concerning the night-time activities at the house and no one seemed any the wiser that De Quincy had been an occasional client. Barbara had imagined that his personal life would have been fully looked into.

But De Quincy, playing by her rules, had been more than careful. He worked in London during the week but now and again he would drive back to enjoy an hour or so of Emma's company. It was not that long a journey and he could be back in town by the early hours.

Why here? Barbara had asked herself when an established client had mentioned De Quincy's possible interest. She liked to know a little of their backgrounds before they were allowed admittance. Why not London where there was far more choice and far less chance of being found out? She was aware he had a girlfriend in Rickenham.

De Quincy had come up with a feeble excuse about the place being more discreet and not wanting his City friends to know but Barbara, an excellent judge of character, saw at once that this was a man who lived for risks, that his main pleasure came not from what he was doing but from the fact that he was doing it so close to home.

When his name had been released as that of the victim she had believed it was all over, that the police would be swarming all over her, because surely even Danny Cotton wouldn't have been able to remain silent under the circumstances. But he had done. They would not make the connection now. Exhausted, Barbara turned out the light and closed her eyes.

Inspector Short drove out to Rickenham General with the intention of having a word with Andy Hicks, the man whom Jimmy Hudson had decided to relieve of some of his blood. He found a space in the vast car-park, grumbling to himself because he had to pay for the privilege of being there.

Making his way towards the main entrance he read what seemed to be innumerable green and white signs all of which pointed in different directions. At the main desk he asked which ward Hicks was in. The hard-faced woman behind it fiddled about with a computer whilst Short watched the comings and goings and chewed his moustache. Finally the woman shook her head. 'He was discharged from casualty with an out-patient's appointment.'

Oh, great, he thought. 'Can you give me his address, please?' It would save contacting someone at headquarters. He produced his identity before the expression of shocked indignation had completely taken hold and was surprised when she complied with his wishes.

Andrew Hicks lived in one of the council houses which looked down over Rickenham. 'It would be the other bloody side of town,' Short muttered. As he made his way out of the building the sky darkened and the first spots of rain began to fall. 'Oh, wonderful,' he said, eyes skyward as he gripped the front of his shabby raincoat and pulled it tightly over his paunch.

Andy Hicks was at home, his wife, Vanessa, said when she opened the door and stood, hand on hip, a question in her uplifted eyebrows.

A very tasty piece, Short thought, his eyes travelling from her high-heeled shoes to the tight, tight skirt in stretchy material. Long blonde hair with only a hint of darker roots hung raggedly over her shoulders. Her make-up was overdone but sexy. She looked about sixteen. 'May I speak to him?'

She inclined her head as if to say, Follow me. Three short steps later they were in the front room. The curtains were drawn and the television was on. Heat came from an electric fire which was too big for the grate and half rested in front of it. Andy Hicks was sprawled on the settee, his injured arm bandaged and in a sling.

'How're you feeling?' Short asked after he had introduced himself. Sexy little Mrs Hicks had made no effort to do so. She had simply thrown herself into the armchair and fixed her eyes on the television screen.

'How do you think? It hurts like hell.'

'Can you tell me what happened exactly?'

'I was on my way to the match when that little heap of shit stabbed me.'

'He says he was provoked,' Short said from his awkward position of being the only one standing and half to the side of Hicks because if he moved he would block Vanessa's view of the television.

'And that makes it all right, I suppose.'

One of those, Short thought. Sullen and uncooperative. Ah, well. He was, he realised, a handsome boy, or would have been had he smiled more readily. Fair hair cut in a modern style, good body and clear skin. All in all a good-looking couple. 'Look, we've got him in the cells. All we need is for you to tell us what happened.'

'Make some tea, Ness. I'll let you know when we want it.'

'I'm watching this.'

Andy Hicks sat upright and got to his feet. He took two strides across the vividly patterned carpet and switched off the set without saying another word.

'Bastard,' Vanessa hissed, but got up and left the room, shutting the door with a crash.

John Short realised that there might be more to the incident than a bit of football hooliganism if Hicks was so determined to speak to him alone.

'What did he tell you? Hudson?'

'You know him?'

'Yeah. Since we were at school.'

'That he was provoked.'

'You already said that. What else?' Andy sat down again, holding the bandaged arm in his other hand.

'That you made fun of his shirt.'

'He told you that?' Hicks' laugh was incredulous. 'He's a liar, then.'

'Oh?'

'It was nothing to do with football.' He paused, wondering whether to go on. 'Shit. You might as well know. It was her fault.' He nodded backwards to where Vanessa had made her exit. 'She's like that, nothing but trouble, always winding me up if she thinks I'm not paying her enough attention. She told me Hudson had made a pass at her, that he said he was really keen and wanted to meet her on the side.'

'Go on.'

'Yeah, well. I saw Hudson and I told him he'd better watch himself. That if I heard anything more like that he'd be sorry.'

'So you threatened him?'

'You could put it that way.'

'When was this?'

'Saturday. Last Saturday morning.' He grinned. 'I obviously scared him because he didn't turn up for the Rickenham cup match that day.'

'You didn't scare him enough, then, not if he came after you with a knife.'

'That's probably why he was carrying it. He'd had time to think about it and he knew I'd break his legs if he wasn't armed. He's a coward, any fight he's in he starts, but he only picks on weaker people, people on their own. I thought I'd got it sorted, I really didn't imagine he'd come after me with a knife.'

So they had been wrong again. None of this was to do with football or the Norwich City shirt Hudson had been wearing.

'I want you to drop the charges.'

'What? I think they must've given you some pretty strong pain-killers.'

'No. I mean it. If it goes to court I'll refuse to appear.'

Short knew what that meant. On such a charge the case would be thrown out, it would not be worth subpoenaing him and if he did turn up a reluctant witness was of no use. 'Why?'

'Because she started it.' He thumbed with his good hand in the direction of the kitchen. 'None of it would've happened if she'd kept her mouth shut. It wasn't true, anyway. She's a bloody liar. I wouldn't have threatened Hudson if she hadn't made it up.'

'How do you know that?'

'I thought about it and I suddenly realised I'd never seen or heard of Hudson having a girlfriend. I asked around, okay?'

'No, it's not okay. I'd like you to explain.'

'Jimmy Hudson's never fitted in, right? Always manages to get himself in trouble by pretending he's a hard man. He isn't. He's a loner and the reason he's a loner is because he isn't like the rest of us.'

'Meaning what?' Short was beginning to respect Andy Hicks. He seemed to have his head screwed on and did not want to make unnecessary trouble.

'He's queer. Gay. Call it what you like, so he couldn't have made a pass at Ness. He's got enough problems, let him go.'

'How did you find this out?'

'A girl I know. Well, I used to go out with her, but for God's sake don't let that be known. She knows him really well, he talks to her. She said she's the only one he can talk to. He knows what he is, the thought of a woman makes him feel sick but he hasn't got the guts to find a bloke because he's terrified of what they call "coming out".

'She made me swear I wouldn't tell anyone, and I haven't apart from you. I should have known, it wasn't the first time Ness has pulled a trick like that. Anyway, that's it. You can tell him what I've said, about not holding any grudges. Do you really want any tea?'

'No thanks.'

'Good. There's football on in a minute. Ness,' he called, getting up to open the door. 'You can bring the tea in now. Just two cups, the inspector's leaving.'

And with that cursory dismissal, Short found himself back outside. Was Andy Hicks straight or did he simply want Hudson on the streets so he could repay the compliment? Time would tell.

When he got back to the station he learned that all the football trouble-makers on the list the computer had produced had been eliminated from the inquiry. It didn't surprise him, that was the way this case was going. When he added his own information there was a groan. They had been looking in the wrong direction. There seemed to be no connection to football at all. In fact, Short decided, on hearing what little progress had been made, there seemed to be no connection to anything. It reminded him of the lottery symbol, as if a hand had reached down from the sky and wiped out two men for no apparent reason.

'It's me,' Ian called as he opened the kitchen door. There was no reply. But the lights were on, Moira was at home. The front room was empty so he went upstairs. His wife was lying in the bath, a glass of wine by the taps and a novel in her hands. 'It's all right for some,' he said, smiling, before kissing the top of her damp head. How slim she is, he thought, she might almost be a young girl. Although, over the years, her skin had coarsened slightly Ian did not notice this. He still saw her as he had on the first day he had met her.

'I didn't expect you so early. I'm getting out now, the water's nearly cold. Pass me that towel.' The water was far from cold but she had had her fill of the green paint. She pulled out the plug and the pipes gurgled noisily, the sound familiar to them both. The plumbing at 14 Belmont Terrace had never behaved well.

Ian sat on the lid of the toilet while she dried herself and applied body lotion. Wiping the condensation from the mirror she began to pluck her eyebrows, still wrapped in the towel. Beneath her eyes she dabbed something from a small pot then smoothed moisturiser into her face. He shook his head, amazed, as he always was at the things women were required to do to themselves before putting on their clothes.

'How was it?'

'Work? You may well ask.'

Which, as Moira well knew, meant don't ask. 'We could eat out tonight, if you like. To make up for the other night,' she added pointedly. 'Only I haven't prepared anything, I got straight in the bath when I came home.'

'I give in. Get your clothes on and we'll go right away. It's still raining, by the way.'

Within half an hour they were walking down the road, huddled beneath one umbrella. Rain splashed off it with a gentle patter. Ian seemed to be heading directly for the Taj Mahal. It was some time since Moira had had a curry so she made no objections.

Seated at their usual table they ordered their food. 'How would you feel if you found out I was not just seeing another woman, but spending the weekends with her?'

'You're with me at weekends. Or else you're at work.'

'Moira, don't be so pedantic, you sound like Alan Campbell. This is a hypothetical question.'

'Then there're two sides to it. How about if I was the woman you were spending the weekends with and discovered you lived elsewhere during the week?'

'Quite. But what would you do about it if you found out?'

'Divorce you before you'd finished explaining yourself.'

'Would most women think that way?'

'Most sensible women.' Moira arranged her serviette neatly across her knees as the waiter brought the wine Ian had ordered to the table. He met Moira's eyes and they both smiled. The wine was already chilled but the waiters at the Taj Mahal seemed not to understand the principle of the lined, plastic container which kept it cool. They always added ice.

'Most. But would someone kill the man because of it?'

'Unlikely. The other woman, maybe.'

Which was exactly what Ian had been thinking. He told her about his visit to Anne Morrisson as they waited for their food to be served.

Anne had been shocked to learn of the loan, so shocked and upset that she had offered to produce all her own bank and building society documentation as well as Justin's. She had no idea where the money could be. De Quincy, naturally, had two sets of paperwork and his finances were being investigated thoroughly in case he owed money elsewhere. But it now seemed unlikely.

'She can't come here. She can't. I couldn't bear it,' Anne had cried when Ian mentioned what Charlotte Jones had said. He felt it was only fair to warn her in case the other woman changed her mind about returning to London.

He had been about to leave, satisfied that he had now met the victim's other girlfriend, when Anne had said, 'What am I supposed to do with his post?'

Most people would have felt free to open it because there were so many things to sort out after a death, but, even knowing what

De Quincy had done to her, she still respected his privacy. 'He doesn't get much mail here, only the household bills. He never wrote personal letters.'

'May I see it?'

She had handed him three letters. 'Would you like me to open them?' Anne had nodded. One, as expected by the logo on the envelope, contained a bill from American Express, the second an invitation to the squash club's New Year's Eve party and the third, in an unmarked A4 envelope, was an account from a private firm of bookmakers. Ian had inhaled deeply. Justin De Quincy had died without cashing a cheque for five and a half thousand pounds. This latest surprise had been the final straw for Anne Morrison; she had collapsed on to the settee, tears streaming from her eyes. 'He had all that money yet he didn't settle his debt with his other woman.' Fortunately, it was at that moment that her sister returned from the supermarket and Ian was able to leave, taking the typed statement with him.

What on earth would the two women make of it when they heard how much he really had? There was no will but De Quincy's parents, disgusted by their son's behaviour, had said any money should be divided between the two women. Time would tell if they meant it. And if he had read Anne Morrisson correctly, he would bet that she would insist her rival received an extra ten thousand pounds.

'All these bits and pieces don't add up to much,' Moira commented. 'In fact, they're just the dross of people's lives really. De Quincy was obviously trying to get his hands on as much money as possible to make his escape. Once that child was born there was no way he could have got away with what he was doing.'

What Moira said was true and Ian knew it. He was clutching at straws. In Walters' case there was nothing amiss financially. His salary had been paid into his bank account and their bills were paid by standing order leaving just enough for them to live on, augmented by Pat's part-time job as a cashier in a supermarket.

'Goddammit! There's got to be something,' Ian said loudly enough for heads to turn.

Moira laid a hand on his. 'There will be. It's not quite a week yet. Mark'll be here soon.' As a distraction it did not work. Ian

114

was quiet throughout the meal and Moira wasn't sorry when it was time to go home.

Towards the end of Friday afternoon Markham found himself in the vicinity of Saxborough Road and decided he might as well see if Danny Cotton was around. He had asked him to keep an eye on Andrews. By now he might have something to tell him.

Why does the thought of him disturb me so much? he asked himself. Richie was thinner than when he had first encountered him and there was a wildness about him as if some inner fire was eating away at his flesh.

He came across Cotton in a shop doorway, chatting to the owner. Tiredness showed in his face and the droop of his shoulders gave him a careworn appearance.

'Is something wrong, sir?' he asked.

'Should there be?' Markham instinctively distrusted the man. He did not wait for an answer. 'Richard Andrews. What's he been up to?'

'I haven't seen him around at all.' Danny averted his eyes as he answered. The interview with the Chief was still playing on his mind and the strain at home was so unbearable that he had forgotten Markham's request. And now there was the added problem of Emma. Each day he was more certain that it was her he wanted to be with but his financial position made it impossible and the idea of not seeing the children every day was unthinkable. How stupid he had been to allow Barbara Fletcher to draw him in so subtly.

Jesus, Markham thought, this man couldn't detect shit if he was standing in it. 'You do know where he lives?'

'Yes. I pass the place several times a day.'

'Well, pass it a few more times and let me know what he's up to.'

'I will, sir.' Danny was relieved when Markham turned away abruptly and strode off down the road. He would make sure he watched Andrews now, he desperately needed something to go right in his life and if he could find out what Andrews was up to at least things might improve at work.

Markham stopped at a newsagent's and bought a copy of the

Rickenham Herald, which came out on Fridays. Naturally, the headlines on the front page concerned the two murders. He stood in the shop reading what Martyn Bright's crime reporter had to say then nodded. Good. The barest details. The identities and ages of the men and their domestic situation, without the prurient aspect of Charlotte Jones. The only other information that the general public was given was where the bodies had been discovered and how they had been killed. Bright had heeded the Chief's warning that he did not want either the nurse or Elizabeth Smith to be interviewed by the paper.

Markham stepped out into the street. The changing colours of the traffic lights were reflected in puddles as the rain continued to fall. In the High Street the Christmas lights swung in the westerly wind above the heads of shoppers. The shops were crowded and the streets busy. Markham almost walked into the back of an elderly woman who had stopped suddenly to consult a shopping list. He rolled the paper and stuffed it into the back pocket of his jeans. He rarely bothered to buy it and only occasionally flicked through someone else's copy. Unless something exceptional occurred, the news it contained centred on council matters, charity walks, schoolchildren's achievements and protests by residents. Throw in the occasional octogenarians' diamond wedding anniversary, a smattering of local brides and the sports pages and that was about the extent of it. The two pages devoted to national and foreign news only contained an exact reproduction of what came off the wires.

Markham realised why all this had been going through his mind. Richie Andrews again. Why had he kept all those copies of the *Herald*? They must go back for almost a year. He was no hoarder, the rest of the flat had been free of clutter. The classified pages? It was doubtful. The flat had central heating so he wasn't saving them as firelighters. There had to be a reason. There was always a reason for everything.

Rain trickled down the collar of Markham's leather jacket. His unprotected head was wet. He had never worn a hat in his life. He walked faster, not because the rain bothered him, he was oblivious to it, but because he wanted to forget about Richie Andrews for the moment or even for ever, because he brought back memories of Julie. And two unresolved murders had to take

116

priority over memories. It was the only way he managed to survive.

Inspector John Short had informed his colleagues of the outcome of his chat with Andy Hicks. Jimmy Hudson was going to plead self-defence, so it was up to themselves whether they went ahead. Short's feeling was that if Hicks was subpoenaed he would go along with whatever Hudson said and make it a fifty-fifty case. 'One for the Super to decide. That's what he's there for. I just hope he hasn't got a taste for it – Hudson, I mean,' Short concluded with a quick tug at his moustache. He shrugged. Some you lost, but at least Hudson had been ruled out as a contender for the murders.

DC Brenda Gibbons had been sent to Rickenham General to speak to the nurse who had found Walters. They had hoped that after the shock had worn off she might recall some detail which had seemed unimportant at the time. Like an accurate description of someone she had seen at the scene brandishing a knife, Short told himself cynically. Some chance. But it had been a bitterly cold afternoon, anyone hanging around would have been conspicuous.

Brenda returned to disappoint them. 'She's quite adamant there was no one else around when she took that short-cut. Apart from Walters, that is, who she found on her way back.'

'Is she all right?' It was Alan Campbell who inquired.

'Yes. She's fine now. She told me she's seen death numerous times but it was very different under those circumstances.'

We're talking for the sake of it, Ian thought. Because we all know that there is nothing to say. At least there had not been a third murder and, for reasons unbeknown to them, neither Ian nor Short now believed there would be.

The week had come to an untidy end as, Ian realised belatedly, had his untaken leave. He would have been due back at work tomorrow but at least he now had the weekend off. The lost days could be claimed another time. Mark was arriving tomorrow and he knew he had worn Moira's patience to breaking point enough times in the past. If he was not around when their only child came home she would not forgive him in a hurry.

Short was startled when Ian refused the offer of a drink but the memory of the evening spent in the Crown was too recent. Ian drove straight to Belmont Terrace, for once hardly aware of the queues of traffic as, lemming-like, commuters and shoppers made for home. The rain, as always, exacerbated the length of the queues. No one walked when they could keep dry. Ian's wipers were full on in an effort to keep the windscreen clear. He would almost welcome the cold again rather than what seemed to be turning into an interminable downpour.

The front room curtains were not drawn although the light was on, giving passers-by an opportunity to stare in at Moira's slender figure which was balanced on a chair. Ian grinned. She just couldn't help herself, he thought as he watched her hang the glass baubles on the real fir tree in the bay window. So much for no fuss. He hoped Mark would appreciate her efforts.

Ian found himself looking forward to his son's visit. He sipped a beer and read the paper whilst Moira finished the tree, then they ate. 'I wish you wouldn't worry so much,' he said when she got up immediately her plate was empty.

'I just want to check that the radiator's on in his room. At least it doesn't smell of paint now. I wonder what he'll make of it?'

'He'll think you did it no matter what we tell him.' Moira, he knew, was excited and a little nervous. It was six months since they had seen their son and she was desperate for his home-coming to be perfect.

He arrived in a taxi which brought him from the station. Ian had offered to drive down to London to collect him but Mark had sounded vague about his arrangements.

Moira, unable to keep still since she had woken that morning, heard the rumble of the taxi's engine before it had pulled to a stop and double parked outside the house. She flung open the front door. Tears filled her eyes as she gazed at Mark, taller than ever, still tanned and with his fair hair bleached by the sun.

Mark grinned and ran up the path to hug her. They were standing in the rain, his bags still on the pavement. 'This is silly. Come on in,' Moira said, hoping her few tears had not been noticed. How like his father he is, she thought, even though their hair's a different colour.

There was so much to talk about and it was late when they

118

went to bed. Ian did not mention the cases in which he was involved. His conscience troubled him. It had been too late when he realised that his devotion to work had caused him to neglect his son when he was at the age to need him most.

'It's so strange . . .' Moira began as she and Ian got ready for bed.

'What is? Having him home again?' Ian got into bed and pulled the duvet around his shoulders. It had been a hard week and he had not been aware that, despite the problems encountered at work, he had been anticipating Mark's arrival as much as Moira. But now he was ready for sleep.

'No. Having conversations with him as a man. I feel quite sad, Ian. All that was Mark as a little boy has finally disappeared.'

'I know. Now get in and give your old man a cuddle.'

Moira laughed. 'Old bugger, you mean.' She was referring to a comment of Mark's. 'The old bugger hasn't driven you to drink yet then?' he had asked good-humouredly.

'It's so nice to be appreciated by one's offspring,' Ian said, pulling Moira's warm body closer to his.

Then within five minutes they were both asleep.

9

Within a very short time the Ropers had adjusted to being a family unit once more. With both parents out at work Mark took the opportunity to relax. He read, watched television and jotted down ideas for future work. Sometimes he arranged to meet up with old friends.

Moira was busy during the run up to Christmas. Some of the wealthy clientele who patronised the garage were buying expensive models for their wives or mistresses but as these orders were ready for delivery by the salesmen on the 24th Moira was given the day off. She and Mark spent most of it in the kitchen preparing traditional food. By the time Ian arrived home at seven fifteen, his face grey and haggard, they had already polished off a bottle of wine in an advance celebration.

'God, what a day,' Ian said, slumped into a kitchen chair.

Mark grinned. 'Just like old times.' But he did not continue because he caught the warning glance from his mother.

Not now, Moira thought, please don't let them start tonight. Fortunately the remark did not register with Ian. He got up and went to the fridge and took out a plastic litre bottle of Adnams bitter. It was, after all, he thought, Christmas Eve.

The three of them were seated around the table and although it should have been a happy occasion Moira had to acknowledge that Mark was right; it was just like old times. Irritated that the two men could not show her at least a little courtesy for the effort she had made by making an effort themselves, she almost put on her coat and told them she was going to spend the evening with Deirdre, her best friend. But this, she thought, would be behaving no better than them and Deirdre might be entertaining a man she had taken up with recently, the first in whom she had shown any interest since the death of her husband many years previously.

I suppose they can't help it, Moira told herself. It's always been the same. And Ian had been working too hard, he had been ready for his leave and had sacrificed over half of it. She knew without his saying that they were nowhere near solving the two cases and that the more time that elapsed, the less likelihood there was of this. Over two weeks now and questions were being asked, not only by the Chief Constable but also by members of the public. And Mark – well, he was a man now but he was still young and often tactless. And, Moira reminded herself, he always forgets Ian's fifteen years older than me.

Whatever happened she was not going to put up with the sullen atmosphere which had developed in her kitchen. She got up to open another bottle of wine and filled two glasses before replenishing Ian's tankard with beer. 'To us,' she said, raising her glass and surprising them both. 'And to the women who have so recently lost their men and will be spending their first Christmas without them.' Her words were sincere but she also hoped to shame them, to put their dissatisfactions into perspective.

Ian met her eyes and understood the message. 'To us,' he said, getting to his feet. 'To my lovely wife and my son. Yes, he's definitely my son.' It sometimes shocked him to see himself as a younger man although Mark was much fairer than he had been.

Mark rose too. 'All right, then. To us. To my crabby old man and my rather special mother.'

Moira bit her lip. Once again she had felt as though she might cry.

The ice was finally broken and they spent a couple of pleasant days doing very little other than eating and drinking and playing board games. Deirdre came for drinks, and Doc Harris and Shirley invited the three of them over on Boxing Day evening and then it was over, although life would not revert to normal properly until after the New Year celebrations.

Each day Ian went into work with a desperate hope that something new would have turned up: each day he was disappointed.

That year they had decided to avoid all the departmental parties which Ian hated but at which he sometimes decided to put in an appearance because he felt it was expected of him. And, to save any fuss and then only because Mark was home, they were going to the Crown on New Year's Eve. Admission was by ticket only and the doors would be locked to anyone without one. The price included free drinks from eight until nine and the buffet which Bill Jones and his wife Connie were providing. Ian thought it was a good idea. There would be no elbow to elbow drinking and no trouble, but he had been surprised that Mark had agreed to go with them, imagining that he would want to spend the evening with his contemporaries. Just another way in which I don't understand my son, he thought as he went to his office and studied his post. There was no way he would have wanted to spend New Year's Eve with his parents.

Mid-morning Gina, his secretary, brought him some coffee. He sipped it gratefully as he made two lists. Despite all the technology available, and with people like DC Alan Campbell only too willing to put it to use on his behalf, Ian still preferred the written word. The physical action of writing somehow helped to clear his mind.

'So what have we got?' he said as he tapped his pen on the desk.

De Quincy	Walters
Battered to death	Knifed
Alma Road	Grounds of Rickenham General
Age 28	Age 41

121

Two girlfriends	Wife and daughter
City trader	Hospital porter
No criminal record	No C.R. (dead child?)
Spanner left at scene	Knife left at scene
No fingerprints	No fingerprints
No known criminal associates	Likewise
Very wealthy. But about to disappear?	Financially straight but money tight.

Now that they had gone over De Quincy's telephone betting account records, it was obvious where the money he had invested had come from.

Ian was not sure he understood the intricacies of spread betting but he realised that you could win a fortune if you were lucky. Conversely, if you were unsuccessful you stood to lose a far greater sum than with an ordinary bet where the odds were clearly stated beforehand.

The fact that he had two women fascinated Ian yet, as Brenda had pointed out, this phenomenon was far from rare. The amazing part was that women apparently accepted whatever story was offered to explain weekend and holiday absences . . .

This was irrelevant. He should be addressing his mind to who had killed the man. He allowed the front two legs of his chair to reconnect with the floor then opened the window before lighting a cigarette. Smoking was frowned upon but Ian argued it was preferable to a stressed-out policeman. Pacing the floor, he muttered as he thought aloud. His feet followed the same pattern on the hard-wearing brown cord. At some point Gina reappeared to remove his coffee cup. She eyed the butts in the ashtray with disapproval but said nothing. She saw how the land lay. It was in this moody state that the Chief often drew conclusions. They were not always right, though.

Bored with his own company and the inability to make any sense of the murders, he wandered down to the serious incident room. On the floor were more boxes containing reports. DC Campbell was where he was most happy, tapping away at the keyboard of a computer.

Walters' background had been the easiest to check because he and his family were local and he had never lived anywhere other than Rickenham Green. From whichever angle they looked at his life, there was nothing to find except for the accident that had put him off driving for ever.

De Quincy came from the Home Counties and had enjoyed all the privileges wealth could provide but his parents were sensible people; once he had left university he had been expected to make it on his own rather than rely on them.

So, we know their backgrounds, we know as much as can be hoped for about two total strangers, and there isn't a bloody thing to suggest why someone wanted them dead, Ian thought, unaware that Alan Campbell had stopped tapping away and was staring at the screen. Markham, behind him, was looking over his shoulder.

'Holy shit! You've found what I wanted.'

'What?' Ian hurried around to the other side of the table and joined them. For a second the fact that De Quincy had been fined for speeding meant nothing. He had been travelling up from London when the traffic division had pulled him, recording his speed at 121 mph. Thousands of people were stopped for speeding but was this innocuous fact the connection for which they had been searching? 'Why wasn't this picked up before?' Ian asked.

'We were only looking for criminal offences, sir,' Alan told him. 'It wasn't until Markham suggested I run the names through traffic ones that it turned up.'

What had Markham seen that Ian had missed?

DS Markham, realising an explanation was required, began to offer one. 'I followed your method. A list. I wondered if they had more in common than it appeared and Alan's come up with this.' He indicated the screen. He shrugged. 'Probably means nothing. Men like De Quincy need the ego trip of a fast car and usually can't manage to hold a clean licence.'

Ian, John Short, who had just appeared, and Alan were as startled by the length of Markham's speech as much as by the content. In his case a whole sentence was a rarity. 'All right,' Ian said, 'but what does it tell us? Does it tell us that we're looking for someone who knew both men, that they've been picked on because of these similarities, as nebulous as they are? I hardly think so.'

'Could be that the killer met De Quincy in London, sir,' Alan volunteered. 'Perhaps he even knew about Miss Jones. Then he followed him here, for whatever reason, and discovered the existence of the other woman and somewhere along the line he met Walters.' Alan was babbling and he knew it. Whatever had tried to surface in his mind had now sunk again.

There was a brief silence. 'It doesn't fit,' Short said philosophically as he crossed his arms and rested his plump buttocks on the edge of the desk. 'For God's sake, you don't kill someone for a speeding offence.'

Perhaps you do, Markham thought but did not say. Perhaps that's exactly it. But he was not a man to voice theories, especially when they were as fanciful as this one. Unlike the Chief his brain did not function better when he discussed possibilities with colleagues. He preferred to close his mind completely, like pulling out the plug of a computer terminal, leaving it blank for a future occasion when other ideas would print themselves on its clear surface. When he was alone he would give the matter more thought.

Danny Cotton's Christmas could not have been worse. The tension between him and Jackie had been unbearable and they were both worn out. At least it had not affected the children's enjoyment of one of the highlights of their year.

On New Year's Day, as if he had made honesty one of his resolutions, Danny had sat the boys in front of the television and told them to stay there. Taking Jackie by the arm he had led her to the kitchen and confessed to his affair with Emma.

Jackie's face had been so white he had feared she might faint. 'I knew,' she had whispered. 'I knew.' Then, much louder, she had said, 'But why, in God's name, did you have to tell me?'

Danny had understood what she meant, that until irrefutable proof was at hand she could have gone on pretending everything was all right. 'I don't know,' he had answered when she wanted to know what he intended doing about the situation.

'You're a weak man, do you know that, Danny Cotton? You don't know how to get yourself out of this but you expect me to do it for you. Really you'd like to have us both with the status quo unaltered, that's it, isn't it?' Her anger, and the truth of her words, had stung him although it was justified.

Impossible to explain the circumstances under which he had

met Emma. Surely no man was brave enough to admit to his wife that he had fallen in love with a prostitute. It made Danny sick to think of Emma in those terms, but that was what she was. Accepted, she did not walk the streets and she only worked on two evenings a week, but the fact remained that she lay on her back for money.

Patrolling his area on the morning of 2nd January, he saw with sudden clarity that he would never have Emma, not completely to himself, unless he took drastic measures. She had her own flat and a full-time job but if he moved in with her he would have nothing to offer. After ensuring his wife and children were cared for there would be little, if anything, over. He could not bear the idea of Emma continuing at Barbara Fletcher's but he was without the means to persuade her to stop. It was agony now, thinking of her with other men, but he could hardly complain when he had been going home to his own family. Now it looked as if he had lost everything.

'Whatever happens, I'll expect you to look after the children,' Jackie had told him. 'Any other time, Danny, and I'd have got a job. But now? Now when I'm six months pregnant?' Her words still rang in his ears.

And Jackie had made the decision for him. She had asked him to leave and not to return until he had sorted himself out one way or another. In desperation he went to Emma's flat which was situated over a baker's in the High Street. There was no reply when he rang the bell. He did not know that she had gone to her sister's for the New Year and was not due to return until that afternoon. He stood staring up at the front windows, behind which was the bedroom that had been the scene of their passion since he had stopped going to Barbara's so frequently. The smell of warm bread made him want to cry. It evoked such strong memories of Emma.

Later, unable to keep away, Danny went back to the town centre. The sales were in full swing and the High Street was crowded. He would not be conspicuous in his uniform, no one questioned the presence of a police officer. Last night he had slept in one of the rooms behind the police station which were reserved as temporary headquarters for officers. Tonight, with a bit of luck, he would share Emma's bed. I've got to speak to her, he thought, it's the only way I'll be able to decide what to do. He

125

had to sort it out for Jackie's sake as well as his own. If Emma admitted that she loved him as much as he loved her then he would leave Jackie for good whatever the consequences.

This time Emma answered the door but her welcome was cool. 'I haven't been in long. Aren't you on duty?' she asked.

'It's all right. Everything's quiet.'

She sighed. 'You'd better come in.'

Upstairs his frown deepened as he watched her unpacking the clothes she had taken with her including, he noticed, a sexy evening dress. He had not known she was going away.

'Emma,' he began.

Ten minutes later neither work nor Richie Andrews mattered any longer.

2nd January. It was all over. Christmas, that is, Ian thought thankfully. Some people dreaded the long, dreary drag until the first signs of spring appeared, but not Ian. He enjoyed having the pubs and restaurants to himself and, by dint of ignoring Christmas and not spending extravagantly as his friends and colleagues did, he and Moira were able to afford to take advantage of those venues throughout January and February. Others would be groaning as their credit card statements fell through the letter-box. The extras provided for Mark's benefit this year had been paid for by Moira.

Mark had left at the same time as Ian had set off for work. He had an afternoon flight to Naples and had seemed half sorry, half glad to be leaving. Moira had wanted to know if he had a girlfriend to which Mark had replied that he did.

'Italian?' Ian had asked with horror, his xenophobia surfacing before he could inquire more tactfully.

'No.'

Ian's relief was short-lived when Mark told him she was French.

Ian was not optimistic. During his break nothing new had come to light and, despite Alan Campbell's over-conscientious attempts to connect De Quincy's speeding offence with Walters' more serious accidental killing of little Alice, no amount of cross-referencing came up with anything else. Meanwhile the painstaking task of sifting through all the evidence for a second time began. That afternoon Brenda Gibbons and Markham were to speak to the men's families again. Christmas may have thrown up a card from a friend or relative whom they had forgotten, one who held a grudge or had the acquaintanceship of both families in common. They were simply going through the motions but anything was worth a try.

Markham was fuming. Not once had Danny Cotton reported back to him and this lack of communication required looking into. And now, it seemed, no one knew where the man was.

At twelve thirty, for want of a better idea, Ian invited John Short to join him for lunch at the Feathers.

'I thought you used the Crown,' he commented, already half-way into his coat.

'Not always. The beer's better there, and the food, but I fancy a change.' It was as if by altering his own routine he could manufacture a breakthrough.

They strolled up the High Street, dodging the bargain hunters. The Christmas lights were still in place and usually remained so until long after the 6th although they were no longer lit by then. Above the buildings patches of blue sky appeared between white clouds but a keen wind blew in their faces.

The pub was busier than either of them had anticipated so early in the New Year. Ian ordered a pint of Guinness because there was no real ale and Short followed his lead. The pub was mock Victorian with all the usual trappings of the era although the carpet was now worn and greasy in places. They sat at a round table with heavy iron legs and waited for their food; ham, egg and chips for Short and lasagne and salad for Ian. A woman on a table near them coughed pointedly and flapped her hand around her head when both men lit up. 'The pub is almost the last bastion of smoking,' Ian said angrily, 'and some silly bitch always has to make a fuss.' He didn't care if she heard him.

Short looked across and smiled at the woman, who seemed to be waiting for someone by the way she kept watching the door. She looked away, repelled by him. 'Can't win 'em all,' Short said. 'I don't think she fancies me.'

They sipped in silence, absorbing the smoke and the smell of food and the rattle of conversation and money as the fruit machine paid out. There was the chink of cutlery on plates as customers who had arrived earlier finished their meals.

127

Short sighed and looked at the froth which lined his glass. 'Could be better. A really decent pint leaves the sides clear.' Ian nodded his agreement. 'Beats me, this murder business. We've looked at every angle, from football violence to jealous women, from domestic to random. No one found that nutter yet?'

'You would have been told if they had.' Over the Christmas period there had been several more complaints of a man fitting the same description.

'I know. Keep your shirt on. I'm simply trying to make conversation until you decide to buy me a drink. Do you think they've forgotten us?' The meal was taking a long time to arrive.

Ian stood and fumbled in his pocket for money. 'No, there's still another couple to be served before us.'

When the meal came it was edible, but only just. Both men left some food on their plates and made their way back to the station.

Sergeant William Baker, known to everyone as Bill, was on the desk when they returned. He was renowned for his hypochondria but nevertheless well liked. 'Sir, I think you're wanted downstairs. They've arrested someone who might just fit the bill. They picked him up by the junction of Ashfarm Close and Churchill Way. He was brandishing a knife and saying he'd killed them.'

Ian took the stairs two at a time, closely followed by Short who felt the discomfort of greasy chips in his stomach as he moved.

On the basement level the cafeteria was to the right, through a pair of swing doors painted bright blue. Today, to add to Short's queasiness, the ever-present aroma of bacon and filter coffee was overridden by the smell of left-over fried fish. To the left, and reached via two echoing corridors set at right angles, was the custody suite.

The custody officer had obviously decided that the presence of a police surgeon was necessary. There were several upon whom they could call; local GPs who took blood tests and patched up minor injuries or attended the scene of a death merely to pronounce the victim dead, whether it be from natural, accidental or murderous causes. The more exciting bits were done by police experts, which Doc Harris who now stood waiting for them resented because he was, at heart, a frustrated pathologist but had only realised this too late in his career to change course.

'I've been advised not to enter alone,' the rotund, gnome-like doctor informed them as he removed his spectacles and rubbed his eyes. Two uniformed officers approached as he spoke.

'Okay. There're enough of us now. Let's go.' Ian rubbed his hands together, body language Doc Harris had come to recognise well. He smiled to himself. Ian was not only going to accompany him, he couldn't wait to get in there.

'Name?' Ian asked belatedly, over his shoulder.

The custody officer's expression was deadpan as he said, 'Gurth.'

Ian stopped and turned around fully. 'Gurth?'

'Just Gurth, sir.' He shook his head. 'That's all he'd say.'

'Doc?' Ian asked as they made their way to the cell. James Harris had had the advantage of a classical education. The name, which to Ian sounded like that of a Scandinavian mythical figure, might mean more to his friend.

'You don't know?' The Doc's eyes gleamed with amusement as he looked up at his considerably taller friend.

'No,' Ian snapped, 'or I wouldn't be asking.'

'Unless I'm mistaken and it really is his name, he's taken it from *Ivanhoe*. The character is a swineherd. Have you really never read it? I thought everyone had.'

My God, Ian thought, ignoring the slight put-down, what sort of creature are we facing?

They waited for the custody officer to unlock the door then the two constables, Doc Harris and Ian stood almost in a line just inside the room. Short elected to remain outside for fear of overcrowding the cell. Seated on the unmade bunk was an immense man with a mane of tangled black hair and a matching beard. Rolls of flesh rippled as he breathed and his clothing was none too clean. Even Scruffy Short looked respectable by comparison. The weather had greatly improved since those bitter weeks before Christmas but it was by no means warm enough for the outfit Gurth had chosen to wear. The black T-shirt had 'Same shit, different day' emblazoned in Day-glo pink on its front and his Union Jack shorts stretched threateningly across his massive thighs. He wore trainers, the laces having been removed, with no socks, and the cell smelled of feet.

The huge head lifted slowly and they saw the glint of a silver crucifix dangling from one ear. Gurth interlaced his fingers, each bearing a tattooed letter which had blurred with age. He smiled benevolently at this unexpected company.

Ian broke the silence by introducing himself. 'And this is Dr Harris. We'd like him to take a look at you, with your permission,' he added sensibly.

Whatever mayhem Gurth had caused prior to his arrest, he now appeared affable and calm, but they were not taking any chances. A man his size could inflict an awful lot of damage if he was upset. But he simply nodded and lay full length on the bed, his arms flung out to the side as if in supplication. So this, Ian thought, is the nutter people have been complaining about. No wonder they noticed him.

As one, the four men moved in closer in case Gurth decided to take the Doc by surprise and crush him to death in his white arms which were larger than most men's thighs.

Ten minutes later, having also taken a sample of blood, the Doc seemed satisfied and they left the cell. 'You won't need the result of the blood test for me to tell you he's on something. Might be dope or something stronger, or even drugs prescribed for psychosis, but you only had to see his pupils and behaviour to tell. Better keep an eye on him. He might start coming down from whatever heights he's reached. Apart from that, despite his bulk, everything else seems to be in working order.'

'Thanks.' Ian wondered whether it would be best to interview him immediately rather than wait for what might be a violent interlude. He summoned the two constables. He and Short would conduct the interview but he wanted help at hand should it prove necessary. 'Gurth,' he muttered. 'What a bloody stupid name.' The Doc's surprise at his lack of literary knowledge still rankled.

The knife had been removed from the prisoner, as had anything else with which he might cause harm either to himself or to others. Both Ian and John Short were more than relieved that this was a requirement before locking someone in a cell.

Big? Short was thinking. The various citizens who had rung in to complain that there was a madman shouting abuse and behaving in a threatening manner must be masters of litotes. The man was enormous.

They went to an interview room and waited for Gurth to be escorted in with a duty lawyer who had arrived remarkably quickly and had had a chance to speak to him briefly. The chair creaked as it took his weight. He listened attentively as the procedure was explained. 'Do you understand what I've been saying?' Short asked.

'My name is Gurth. My vocation is swine. Pigs, you understand, although I mean no offence to anyone here. I round them up and, like a farmer, I single out the ones ready to be killed. They are not always the fattest ones but they are the bad ones, the rogue animals, the ones who do society harm. My vocation is similar to your job except you do not have the power to punish, only to detain or arrest. When I explain what I do you will be grateful to me and let me go.'

He's psychotic, Ian thought.

Raving bonkers, Short decided, before settling back in his chair with his arms folded to hear what else was coming.

Half an hour later Ian shook his head. They were getting nowhere. Gurth refused to give any other name and only reiterated that his role was to weed out the bad ones and thus make the world a better place. We need a psychiatrist, Ian decided.

The duty solicitor had said very little, probably, Ian realised, because he was as dumb-struck as they were. They had kept strictly to the rules and Gurth, despite his ramblings, seemed to be intelligent.

'Did you kill Justin De Quincy and David Walters?' Ian had asked.

'I told you I kill rogue pigs.'

This was not an admission and, without a psychiatric report, no admission would be worth a thing anyway. They were about to give up and have Gurth taken back to his cell when a gentle tap on the door interrupted them. Short went to see who wanted them. A lumpy WPC stood there with a worried look on her face and a note in her hand. 'Can you give this to the Chief, please?'

Short took the note and read the few lines written on a sheet of ruled paper torn from a shorthand pad.

Gurth, still smiling amiably, was led away leaving Ian to muse over ways in which they were likely to get any sense out of him. There was nothing amongst his few possessions which hinted at his real identity. Would even a psychiatrist be able to get at the truth? If Gurth was way beyond the realms of sanity it might be that his guilt or innocence would never be known.

'Ian,' Short interrupted, 'we seem to have here what is commonly known these days as a hostage situation.'

'What?' Ian's head jerked around, his eyes wide with surprise.

'Mmm. Afraid so. A woman's being held at knifepoint above a shop in the town centre.'

Knifepoint. Ian's stomach contracted. Had the murderer, assuming the weirdo in the cells was not their man, decided to strike again and been disturbed? Was he holding the woman as his get-away insurance? 'Right. Who've we got?'

Short understood the question. Certain people in the division had been hand picked to attend courses where they were trained how to act in special circumstances. They would be pulled off whatever they were involved in at the time if these circumstances arose. 'Dean Curry and Brenda Gibbons.'

Brenda. Of course. Ian had almost forgotten she had been on the course and had already had the opportunity to put it to practical use. But that had all happened before she joined them at Rickenham Green.

Markham, they learned, on his way back from seeing Anne Morrisson, had come across two patrol cars slewed at one side of the High Street. It was already getting dark, and the blue lights swirling silently had added to the confusion which, for a split second, led Markham to believe that the cars had collided. As soon as he saw the crowd on the opposite side of the pavement staring at an upstairs window he knew something serious was on. One officer was half sitting in his car, his feet resting on the pavement as he spoke on the two-way radio.

Markham asked him what was happening then used his mobile phone to get a message through to the Chief in case the earlier one from the patrol car had not yet reached him.

'Get Markham back on the phone,' Ian instructed John Short. He did so, not in the least offended at the Chief's tone.

'He's armed,' Markham said. Then added quietly, 'We can't use Brenda. She knows him. It's PC Cotton up there. Danny Cotton.'

'Oh, shit! We'll have to use Curry. Does he know Curry?'

'I don't know, but I doubt it.'

It went through their minds that Cotton had cracked up, that the reason he had had difficulties with the job was because of the stress he was under at home. Until lately, as community officer, he seemed to have pulled himself together but, according to rumours, he had been slipping again. Two people were dead and a third was in danger. If Cotton was responsible all hell would break loose. It was not all that long ago that one of their own had murdered his wife. And only recently Cotton had been under suspicion for another reason.

Within minutes it seemed as though half the division were on the doorstep of the baker's shop, as well as the staff. With the arrival of assistance the street was cordoned off and cleared of pedestrians. The two constables at the top of the flight of wooden stairs which led to Emma Drew's flat had made only one attempt to talk Cotton out. They were not experts and could have made the situation worse. Instead, they told the man inside, whose identity they were as yet ignorant of, that someone was on their way to talk to him, to help him if possible. All they could do then was to wait and guard the door in case he tried to escape. There was no other way out unless he decided to jump from a back window into the alley which was blind at one end and had a police officer at the other.

Ian's driver had made the journey as fast as was safe. The car had not quite stopped moving when Ian threw himself out of it. 'Anything happened?' he asked Markham, who was leaning against the side of the patrol car, his hands on its roof.

'No. Everything's gone quiet. Woman from the bakery heard screaming. She knows the girl up there.' He nodded towards the open street door which was sandwiched between the plate glass windows of a shoe shop and the bakery. 'That's why she rang us. She said there's never been any noise or trouble before and the screams frightened her.'

'How do we know it's Cotton? Did the response team tell you?'

'No. I saw him in the window. Only briefly, but it's him. Still got his uniform on. I wanted to speak to him myself but no one had seen him since this morning. Looks like he didn't do his rounds this afternoon.'

'Let's hope they get him out soon.'

As they waited for the arrival of Dean Curry, Brenda Gibbons was making her way back from Pat Walters' house. It had been a wasted forty minutes. She saw the commotion ahead of her and had to produce her identity before the police diverting the traffic would allow her through. Leaving the car in a side road she walked down the virtually deserted street. The Chief's head was visible over those of the people surrounding him. Not another murder, was her first thought.

Having been given a quick explanation Brenda bit her lip, disappointed that she was not to be the one to go up there. Accepted, the odds were hard to assess. Did you send someone of the same or the opposite sex to negotiate? It could work for and against, as could the fact that she knew Danny Cotton, albeit not well. Perhaps a stranger was better.

Dean Curry held the rank of inspector. He was lean with a deceptively boyish face and a clean-cut look, but he was an experienced officer and a good negotiator. 'His name's Daniel Cotton. Danny to his friends,' Ian briefed him. 'Unfortunately he's one of us.'

There was no sign of recognition in Curry's face. 'And the girl?'

'Emma Drew, according to the manageress of the bakery. At least, that's who lives there and she saw her coming back with an overnight bag sometime after lunch. Go on, see what you can do.' Ian turned to see Markham in discussion with a middle-aged woman in a pink and white checked overall. On her head was a white cotton cap. He went to join them.

'Mrs Jackson,' Markham said. 'The lady who rang us. She says Emma came into the shop and bought a loaf of bread before she went upstairs, that's how she knew she was home.'

'I heard her go up the stairs,' Mrs Jackson added, breathless to repeat her story.

The two men let her continue. There might be discrepancies in her second account and they did not want another Elizabeth Smith on their hands. It was Martyn Bright who was having to deal with her now. He had told them she rang the paper almost daily wanting to know what was happening and why the police hadn't caught anyone. And then, as if the thought had crossed their minds simultaneously, they stared at each other. They both realised that they might have misjudged her, that she might, in fact, have really seen more than she had told them initially. Because Danny Cotton had a moustache.

'She wasn't back long,' Mrs Jackson continued. 'Fifteen minutes, twenty at the most, I heard her doorbell. It's by the street

134

door. She came down and two of them went up. The stairs run up along the wall behind the counter, that's how I know. It was all quiet after that. Mind you, you can't hear anything from upstairs unless the shop's quiet, and only creaking and suchlike then. I heard those screams though. That poor girl's scared to death, take my word for it.'

Markham nodded. The script had not altered from the first telling. 'And you didn't see who it was?' She could hardly have missed the uniform if she had seen him.

'No, love. Not from where I was standing.' Mrs Jackson moved away to gossip with the two women with whom she worked.

Brenda Gibbons, chewing a thumbnail, took it all in from the doorway of Emma's building, wishing she was upstairs.

'How did the response team gain entry?'

'She didn't lock the street level door after she let him in. The flat has its own front door at the top of the stairs.'

Did Cotton know the girl? Ian wondered, But of course he knew her. You did not let a stranger into your home then sit and chat, or whatever they had been doing before he produced the knife. Ian went back to the car and radioed the station. 'Alan, check this out, will you? See if Daniel Cotton has ever had reason to speak to De Quincy and his girlfriend or the Walters. And get someone to find out if either of the two women have ever heard of a girl called Emma Drew.'

'How do we know he's got a knife?' Ian inquired when he walked back to where Markham was standing.

'Constable Stone, the first officer on the scene, spoke to him. Cotton told him so and the girl confirmed it.'

There was still no sign of Curry. Part of his role was to make it perfectly clear that he did not have the authority to grant any of Danny's requests, that he had to discuss them with his superiors. And they always did want something even if they didn't always know what it was. Sometimes a lifetime of deprivation and frustration caused people to take a hostage as a way of saying, 'I'm me, I'm alive, I exist. There has to be something better than this.' Was that the case with Danny Cotton? A man destined never to gain promotion, a man with a wife and small children for whom he would have to provide for the next sixteen years at least? Then there was Barbara Fletcher. Danny had as much as admitted he was having a fling with her. In which case, who, exactly, was Emma? That question could wait, for now her safety was paramount.

Inconspicuously, marksmen had taken up their positions, their weapons aimed at the front window of the flat. It was now completely dark and the scene was eerie. Shop lights spilled out on to the pavements but the premises were empty. No illegally parked cars lined the sides of the road, apart from a couple of police vehicles. The rest had been moved out of sight so as not to intimidate Cotton. Ian knew he must do something about allowing the shopkeepers to lock up properly. He was about to ask Brenda to organise this when Curry reappeared, his young-looking face was serious. 'It's no good, he won't say what he wants or what he wants us to do.'

'And the girl?' Let this be over quickly, Ian prayed. Let him come out of his own accord. He was fully aware of the danger of storming the place but they couldn't have the town centre disrupted for days. The part of the bathroom window which opened was too small to allow entry. The bedroom window was the sash type but the glass would have to be smashed and that wasn't on. Besides, to reach it meant using a ladder which would clatter or lowering someone from the roof by means of a rope. They could not get in without Cotton hearing them which would give him vital seconds in which he could inflict damage.

'She's alive, but she isn't saying much either. He won't let her talk.'

'Okay. Do you want to try again?'

'I think you might have better luck with DC Gibbons. A new approach might help.'

Brenda concealed the triumph she felt. If she was successful it might add weight to her next application for promotion. She was determined to make it and she had recovered from the Chief's unintentional slap in the face when he had told her that he would not recommend her for promotion yet because he did not feel she was ready for it. He had been right. She had learned a lot during the past months and had settled down emotionally. How much of this was due to her relationship with Andrew Osborne, she wasn't sure.

Breathing deeply she mounted the stairs, ensuring her footsteps were heard. Then she cleared her throat loudly. There must be

no sudden surprises to startle either of the occupants of the room.
'Hello?'

'Who's there?'

'Brenda Gibbons, Danny. You know me.'

'What do you want?'

Most people would have replied that what he wanted was
more to the point, but rule number one was always answer the
questions and never, ever lie. 'We want you and Emma to come
out unharmed. What can we do to ensure that?' We, let him
know from the start. As her nervousness disappeared all her
training came back to her.

'Brenda? Can I call you Brenda?'

'Yes, of course.' I've got him, she thought. It was the beginning
of the bond of trust which had to be created before any progress
was made.

'I've fucked up, haven't I?'

'You've got problems, I'll give you that, Danny.' Change the
subject fast, girl, those sort of questions I can do without, she told
herself. 'Is Emma all right?'

'I've got nothing left now. No job, no wife, no nothing.'

'Is Emma your girlfriend?' Brenda wanted to talk about his
wife but she did not want to make him angry. Did she know?
Had anyone contacted Jackie Cotton yet?

'Not any more.'

'Then why not let her go? Your wife will be wondering where
you are. Do you help her put the children to bed?'

'Doesn't she know what's happened?'

'I can't tell you that, Danny. I don't know if they've managed
to get hold of her.'

'Perhaps she needn't know.' Danny sounded unrealistically
relieved. Jackie would take him back as long as she didn't find
out. No one knew she had thrown him out. He had used some
other excuse for staying in a room at the station last night.

Brenda realised how disturbed he was. Any policeman would
realise it was impossible for his wife not to find out.

'Why do you need the knife, Danny? Emma can't hurt you,
surely? Not a man with your strength and training.'

'I was going to kill us both.'

Brenda's mouth was dry. I was going to. Past tense. 'Jackie'll
be worried. Open the door, Danny. Let Emma go and we'll see if

137

we can sort this out. Would you like to speak to your wife if we can find her?'

Without warning the door was flung open and a pretty but grey-faced girl was pushed roughly out on to the small landing, almost knocking Brenda over. 'Go on down,' she whispered unable to even offer the girl a hand because Danny had slammed the door shut and was still in there armed with a knife. He had to know how bleak his future was, and the next few minutes were vital if he was to be prevented from taking his own life. 'Danny, you've already made things better for yourself, but this is Emma's flat, you can't stay in there indefinitely. Do you need anything to eat or drink? I can arrange it. Danny?' Keep calm, she told herself, keep perfectly calm. 'Danny,' she repeated more loudly, 'will you please answer me?' She counted to ten and tried again. 'Oh, God, no,' she whispered as she raced down the stairs. 'Break the door down,' she yelled at Ian.

'Go,' Ian ordered.

Two of the tactical force team ran up the stairs. The crack as the door frame gave could be heard in the street.

An ambulance had been standing by. Markham waved it towards him from where it had been parked out of sight of the flat window. It drifted to the kerb by the bakery just as Danny Cotton was being half carried, half dragged down the stairs, blood leaving darker stains on his uniform. He had had to be restrained to allow the paramedics to bandage his wrists and administer sedation. Two officers accompanied him to Rickenham General.

'Well done, Brenda.'

'Thank you, sir.' She was sitting on the edge of the pavement, her feet in the road, her arms hugging her body as though she was freezing. Lifting her head, Ian saw the tears in her eyes but they did not fall. 'Will he live?'

'I expect so. They got to him quickly, thanks to you – he won't have lost all that much blood.'

Brenda nodded. She knew that spilled blood always gave an exaggerated idea of the severity of an injury, that a quarter of a pint could seem like a gallon when it seeped into clothing. Emma was safe but she had wanted them both out of that building unscathed. How stupid she was to aim constantly for perfection when what really mattered was that two lives were no longer at risk. The striving to prove something was exhausting and she wondered if it would ever end. Maybe time and Andrew Osborne would provide the answer. The burning anger she had lived with for years had disappeared and she no longer blamed an alcoholic mother and an absent father for her lack of self-esteem. And the foster parents with whom she had finally been housed had been good to her, she had to remember that. If you can't hack the job, girl, don't do it, she told herself. She stood and straightened her clothes. But I can and I will, she thought with determination as she gave Ian a half-hearted smile. 'What now?'

'Now we wait to see what Cotton has to say for himself. I've asked someone to check his rota for the dates of the murders. And we'll find out what the brain doctor has to say about Gurth.'

'Gurth? Gurth?' she repeated, her hazel eyes wide with amused surprise.

'Ah, you don't know. Then you're in for a treat.'

10

Richie Andrews paced his room. Tomorrow. The word echoed in his head. He was hot, burning with a dry heat although he had opened the window to let in the cold night air. Nothing he ate stayed down so he had given up on food but never had he felt so alive. Everything was ready, he had even paid his rent until the end of the month. All he had to do was to get through the night.

'Markham,' he said, repeating the name over and over again. Then he laughed. 'We have one thing in common. We're loners.' He continued his relentless pacing and thought about Christmas Day.

He had gone to the Black Horse only because it was the nearest pub, and had made three drinks last the whole session. Unlike Martin, he had never been able to hold his drink. Once the family groups had drifted off home for their turkey the remaining customers had been men like himself. 'And you.' Richie laughed again at the thought of Markham propping up the other end of the bar with no one to talk to and no one waiting at home.

Almost starving and without sleep he felt as though he was

floating, that his feet were not making contact with the carpet as he moved around the room. Hatred was a powerful force, and there were two people he hated. He could not bring himself to question how life would be when they no longer existed because without that hate he would cease to exist himself.

As the High Street was reopened to traffic and normality began to return, Brenda accompanied the Chief back to the station, following in her own car. She was exhausted and the night had turned chilly. A hot bath and bed were something to look forward to.

The warmth of the radiators was welcoming, as was the idea of the coffee which Ian suggested.

Victor Thomas was sitting behind Ian's desk, having made himself completely at home. In front of him was a plate containing an empty, rigid sandwich wrapper and a disposable coffee cup. 'Ah, at last,' he said, flicking the switch of the dictaphone. He caught Ian's look of horror. 'Don't panic, I removed your cassette first. This is my own. I thought I might as well make use of the time.'

Victor was a man of middle height with drooping shoulders, a beak-like nose and a fringe of brown hair which framed his otherwise bald head. His age could have been anywhere between thirty-five and fifty. He cocked his head to one side inquiringly upon seeing the attractive figure of Brenda Gibbons behind Ian.

The introductions were made as the coffee arrived. Ian cursed the fact that Gina wasn't on hand at all times to fetch it for him. All three were seated and exchanged a few pleasantries before they got down to business. The office smelt of stale smoke which was only noticeable to Ian if he had been away from it for any length of time. The nicotine had not yet had time to make an impression on the unimaginative décor, which Ian thought was a pity.

'Gurth,' Victor Thomas began as he spooned sugar into his cup, 'is far more straightforward than you might think.' He met Ian's eyes. 'I know you would like him to be your murderer, but I think that's highly unlikely.'

'A possible suspect at the moment, that's all.'

Brenda knew nothing of the occurrences of earlier in the

140

afternoon. Ian suddenly remembered this and explained. When he gave a brief description of his appearance Brenda made the connection. 'He's the man people have been ringing in about.'

'Yes. Sorry, Victor. Go on.'

'Before I spoke to him I made some inquiries. He was an in-patient at Mounthaven for several months. He suffers from visual and auditory hallucinations and my guess is that now, as an occasional out-patient, he forgets to take his medication which is why these outbursts happen.

'People like Gurth – his real name's Robert Bell, by the way – are treated like pariahs. I accept they can appear frightening but they are the ones who are terrified. They live in a doubly populated world, the real one, which we all see and hear, and the other one which their brains are registering but which doesn't actually exist. Can you imagine the clamour? All those people talking at once, real and imaginary? The voices they hear are mostly abusive and derogatory.'

'You're not telling me anything I didn't know here. What're you laying the ground for?'

'That's not my style. I'm simply trying to explain. His consultant at Mounthaven told me that Gurth's an intelligent man and in his case, unusually, his hallucinations are based on experience. When he says he kills pigs, he does just that. In his head, of course.'

'He carries a knife,' Ian pointed out abruptly.

'But as far as we know he's never actually used it. Yes, all right, he waves it about, but that's the extent of it.'

'Oh, well, a harmless occupation, wouldn't you say? Supposing it connects with someone or has already done so? Are you condoning such behaviour?'

'Oh, for God's sake, Ian, don't be so pompous. Of course I'm not. Let me get to the point, if you'll excuse the pun. Gurth's father was a pig farmer. One of these animals turned vicious and was segregated from the rest. Unfortunately it broke loose and attacked the man. He eventually died from his injuries. Gurth witnessed the attack. He was six years old.'

Ian nodded and Brenda closed her eyes. There was nothing they could possibly say.

'So he's being quite literal, you see. When he says pigs he means pigs, not people or the police.'

'Quite.' In Ian's opinion the last phrase had been an unnecessary dig.

'But it could have happened, though only on the assumption that our two cases aren't connected,' Brenda said. She was sitting to one side of Ian, her coat open to reveal a pale lilac sweater in soft wool and a straight, purple skirt. 'Look, some psychiatric patients feel more at home on hospital premises than anywhere else. Supposing he was in the grounds of Rickenham General when he hears these voices or whatever it is he sees appears? He lashes out just as David Walters is coming off his shift.'

Victor rubbed his chin. It was almost as smooth as his head. 'You have a point there, but surely there would have been other people leaving at the same time. Someone would have seen Gurth. I mean, he's not exactly inconspicuous. As I said earlier, in my view the likelihood of him being your man is next to nil.'

Disappointed as he was, Ian could not disagree. 'What's the best course of action now?'

'Have you charged him with anything?'

'No.' And it seemed pointless to do so. He had been creating a public nuisance and carrying an offensive weapon but it was treatment Gurth required, not punishment.

'Well, if it's not blatantly breaking any rules, can you keep him here overnight? I've given him his medication and the custody officer has his morning dose. He's happy enough down there, he'll sleep all right. I'll arrange to have him readmitted in the morning.'

'I need a drink,' Ian said with feeling when Victor Thomas had departed, 'It's been one hell of a day. Care to join me?'

'Sounds like a good idea.' Brenda stood and buttoned her coat. It was black. Ian plucked a long, chestnut hair from her shoulder without thinking, just as he would have done with Moira.

'Where do you fancy?' Ian asked as they stepped out into the blustery street.

'The George?' She knew he favoured the Crown but she would be left stranded when he got into conversation with Bob Jones, the landlord. They turned left at the top of the High Street and walked the short distance to the mock Tudor building. It was a place which catered to the middle-class and lunchtime businessmen and although it was, as Short always claimed, pretentious, at least there was a lack of pool tables and noisy machines and it

142

was comfortable. Where was Short? she wondered. It was a question often on people's minds.

The awful events of the day were put into perspective when she saw, standing at the bar, the familiar and by now dear figure of Andrew Osborne. The Chief would never believe she had not expected to find him here. Well, bugger the Chief, she thought as a smile lit up her eyes.

Andrew Osborne, turning around when he felt the draught from the door, smiled back.

Emma Drew had refused the offer of a check-up at Rickenham General. 'I'm not hurt,' she insisted and still refused when it was pointed out that she might be suffering from shock. 'Really, I'm fine. I'd rather make a statement now and get it over with.'

When she had done so she asked to go home. 'I don't think you ought to go back there tonight, love,' a concerned WPC had told her. 'Can't you stay with a friend until our cleaners go in tomorrow?' Danny Cotton's blood had stained the furniture. By then Emma had to admit she was feeling shaky and agreed. WPC Dollis said she would drive her.

'Let me know where she goes,' Markham said quietly before they left. WPC Dollis nodded. Ten minutes later she radioed in to say she had dropped Emma Drew at 101 Saxborough Road.

Barbara Fletcher's house, as Markham had guessed. He had returned to the station with Emma to take her statement. He now went straight to the incident room to find out if Alan Campbell had come up with the information he wanted. He had. Markham flicked through the telephone directory and found Martyn Bright's home number.

'What? You mean now?' Bright said upon hearing the request made of him.

'I'll owe you one.'

'Roper already owes me one. You lot can consider yourselves deeply in my debt. Look, all right, as long as it won't take more than half an hour. My wife's gone to bed early and she's just dropped off to sleep, the kid's been playing her up all day.'

'Then leave her a note in case she wakes. See you in twenty minutes.' And with that Markham was on his way.

St Luke's clock chimed the half-hour as he strode through the

143

quiet evening streets. It was an incongruous sound since the rapid growth of the town. He turned right into Deben Lane, deserted now because there were no houses here, only a hedge and fields on one side and the flat, open countryside of Suffolk on the other. Further down it became populated and the hedge became a six-foot wooden fence, behind which a housing estate nestled. On the right was a sprawl of low buildings and warehouses, inaptly named the Poplars Business Park. It was a trading estate and the said poplars had been ripped up in order to build it. It was here that the offices of the *Rickenham Herald* had been relocated from the Edwardian fronted premises in Saxborough Road where, for the convenience of local residents wishing to place advertisements, they had retained one room.

Markham considered the possibility of being wrong. He knew that without the slightest trace of evidence his idea would be ridiculed. But he had been involved personally and he, indirectly, might have cost two people their lives. His conscience did not trouble him. He did his job. He was not responsible for the actions of others.

Bright, who had driven, was there ahead of him, standing in the marked-out car-park in front of the two-storey glass-fronted building. He jangled his keys impatiently.

Markham grinned. Bright had always been brash and cocky and had believed himself to be irresistible to women. Once, he might have been, but his 1970s Kevin Keegan hairstyle was dated and the developing paunch spoke more of home cooking than illicit nooky.

'Which years?' Bright asked as he led him through the building, throwing light switches as he went. It produced a ghostly effect. Without the buzz of human occupation and the constant ringing of telephones it seemed strange. The screens on the desks were covered in plastic hoods like so many caged birds tucked up for the night.

'Last year. For the months of February and March.'

'Here, I'll load it.' Bright switched on the microfiche viewer, eager to help now that he knew this wasn't going to take long.

Markham swivelled a typist's chair around and sat astride it, leaning on its back as he flicked through the pages. The front page news of the edition he was scanning concerned the prospective building of a swimming-pool and leisure centre. Half the

144

page was dedicated to a colourful drawing of how the architect saw it. As with many such ideas in Rickenham Green, nothing had been heard of it since. His eyes travelled slowly over the next three pages, then, on page five, he saw it. It was not the initial story of the accident which interested Markham but the report of the hearing which had followed it. And there it was, alongside a photograph of a haggard David Walters and his wife who was clinging to his arm. *Exonerated: but Walters claims he's guilty*, the large caption read. The article more or less reiterated what his wife had told them. Walters claimed that whatever the law might think, he would never be able to forgive himself. It gave his address as Aspen Road, Rickenham Green, but did not include the number. 'Can you run me off a copy?' Bright obliged.

Markham found the second item equally quickly and frowned as he read it. There was no photograph and the non-story warranted only two short paragraphs.

Justin De Quincy, 27, of Crossley Close was stopped for speeding on the A12 at the end of last year as he travelled back from his job in the city. His speed was monitored for over a mile at 121 mph.

De Quincy, who showed negative signs of drinking when breathalysed, was fined and ordered to pay costs.

I was wrong, he decided, having noted the straightforward account of the facts. Then he noticed the bottom line. In smaller print it said, *See editorial comment, page 8.*

He turned to it. Bright was now reading over his shoulder. Basically the article was asking why it was that someone who had money, two homes and an expensive car should get off so lightly when they, with all their advantages, had endangered the lives of others: they ought to be subjected to heavier fines. He was surprised at the judgemental tone of the article but it was far more eye-catching than the account itself.

'I remember that,' Bright said.

'Why?'

'You've seen the paper. It was a sparse week for news. I was pretty desperate to have written that.'

A chain of petty circumstances had led to De Quincy's death. If I'm right, Markham thought. But to be fair, if it hadn't been him it could have been someone else. If I'm right, he thought again. 'Thanks. Can you copy these two pages as well? Then I'll let you get back to your family.'

He had found what he had hoped to find after Alan had dug up the hearing dates. He had known the outcome would have been reported in the following Friday's paper.

He went back to headquarters, quiet now because of the lateness of the hour, although it was still too early for the drunks to be making a nuisance of themselves. He wrote up his notes and left a copy with the file on Short's desk, then he went home.

Sleep eluded Markham too. He knew what tomorrow was and he was certain he now knew the reason that Richie Andrews had remained in Rickenham Green.

Barbara Fletcher was not expecting visitors and she had told the girls they weren't needed until the second week in January. There was never any trade over Christmas and the New Year as even the most remiss of husbands tended to become domesticated for a short period. After the rows caused by enforced proximity broke out they would be back by the dozen.

She heard a car pull in but thought nothing of it. Although the road was marked with double yellow lines people were always stopping to let out or pick up passengers thanks to the number of bed-sits in the area.

The television was off; Barbara was having a quiet evening with a book. On the table beside her was a glass of whisky and soda. When the doorbell rang she frowned in annoyance. One of her clients, no doubt, who had taken it into his head to turn up without an appointment. Seeing Emma with a WPC on her doorstep threw her into an inner turmoil which she hid extremely well. So it's come to this, she thought, smiling because, if necessary, she would lie her head off. She's shopped me and is going off to live happily ever after with that thick PC.

'Barbara, I'm sorry. I didn't have anywhere else to go. Would it be all right if I stayed the night?'

Barbara glanced over her head at WPC Dollis for clarification. Only now did she notice the state that Emma was in. There was no doubt something bad had happened to her.

'There was an incident this afternoon, Mrs Fletcher. Miss Drew was ... well, perhaps it's best if she tells you herself. We won't need to trouble her again tonight.'

'How rude of me. Please, come in, both of you,' Barbara said

146

graciously. They had been standing in full view of passing cars and pedestrians while the wind whipped around them. They went through to the lounge where Barbara offered tea or coffee. WPC Dollis said she could not stay, she had only come to make sure Emma had somewhere to spend the night.

Emma slumped into one of the settees, head bowed, as Barbara saw the other woman out and closed and locked the front door.

'You need a drink, my girl. What'll it be? Um, brandy I think. Want to tell me about it?' she asked over her shoulder as she poured the drinks usually reserved for clients. Now was not the time to mention the fright she had received. It was obvious nothing had been said about the business being done at the house. In fact, it may have worked to her advantage. That young policewoman had stood in her lounge and seen only Barbara, an elegant middle-aged lady, alone and engaged in a totally innocent pastime.

'I've been so stupid,' Emma began as the tears which she had been too numb to shed began to roll down her face.

Barbara went across and sat beside Emma. It took an effort but she held her in her arms, pulling her close, unmindful that some hair had escaped the neat coil into which she she had twisted it and that Emma's tears were staining the silk material of her dress. It had been the same all her life: she had flinched from physical contact except when she had earned her living from it. But somehow that hadn't counted.

Emma sobbed, her shoulders shaking, until she could cry no more. Barbara shushed her and stroked the curly, black hair, thinking of another soft head as she did so. He won't come back, she told herself, as she had done so after that one and only visit.

'Danny was in love with me,' Emma said, sitting up, dry-eyed now but puffy-faced. 'Really in love, I mean. More like an obsession. I shouldn't have done it, let him see me away from this place. But he was young and gentle. I knew he was married but I thought he just wanted some fun until his wife had had the baby. You know how it is.'

Indeed I do, Barbara thought. It is the way in which I make my living.

'Apparently he admitted the affair to his wife and she kicked him out. Strange, I knew immediately he told me that I didn't want to see him again, ever. He was in such a state and he should have been on duty. I let him talk, rant, more like it, for ages. I was wondering how to get rid of him. God, he was acting so strangely. In the end, when he kept on that he couldn't live without me, I decided I had to be blunt. I said I didn't want to see him any more, that his wife needed him and he had to leave. That's when he picked up the knife.

'We were in the kitchen. We'd been there all the time. I've got one of those magnetic things to hold my cooking knives. He grabbed the biggest one and threatened me with it, saying if I didn't want him he'd kill us both. I was terrified, Barbara, but I screamed my lungs out hoping that someone downstairs would hear me. They obviously did. He meant it, he would have killed us if the police hadn't come so quickly. I managed to calm him down. I told him I did love him.'

'Let me get you another drink.' Barbara got up to pour it in the pause which followed as Emma relived her experience silently.

'Thanks. He's mad, you know, totally round the bend.'

'Well, I did wonder if it was Danny who broke in here. Whoever did it certainly knew what they were about and he had been acting rather strangely at the time. Then I realised it wasn't him.' She stopped, unwilling to admit what she had worked out. During the burglary she had lost two of the items that were most dear to her. There was only one person who would have known what they were; the person who would know how to hurt her because she had hurt him.

However, now that Danny was out of the equation, Emma was back on her side. It was to Barbara she had come for help, therefore she was not about to admit anything to the police. What Danny might say was a different matter but he had already proved himself unstable and it would be her and Emma's word against his.

'Danny's got nothing to lose. What if he says something about us?' Emma asked as her thoughts travelled in the same direction. As she leaned forward to place her glass on the table her hand shook violently. Delayed shock had hit her and she felt suddenly cold in the warm room.

'Except any credibility he might have left. If there's any chance of the wife sticking by him he isn't going to lessen it by admitting how he met you. And it's his word against ours. We must warn Molly. I can't recall him meeting anyone here except that once when I wanted him to know what he'd got himself into. We can deny anything you might have told him.' Emma's quick blush told Barbara she had discussed what went on in the house.

The police were not stupid, if you discounted Danny, she thought. They had no suspicions because she wasn't greedy.

Emma had made a mistake, but so had Barbara. It had not been such a good idea to corrupt the local policeman in order to ensure his silence as far as her activities went. In fact, in retrospect, she saw that he could have continued visiting the house and never have noticed that anything was amiss.

11

'Those scarves, Moira. I just don't get it.' Ian was leaning over a kitchen chair, his knuckles gripping the back of it. When his wife did not reply he turned around to see her standing in front of the washing-machine, head bowed and a single sock stretched between her hands. 'Moira?'

'It's Mark's. He must've forgotten it.'

Ian understood. The finding of this small item had emphasised their son's leaving more than the disappearing taxi carrying Mark and his luggage had done. He smiled and reached for her hand.

'No, don't. I'll only start crying if you're nice to me,' she said. 'I'm sorry. What were you talking about?'

'Nothing. Only work.'

'No, go on.' She pulled out a chair and sat down. Anything would be a distraction. In a day or two her maternal longings would have settled down again and she would begin to look forward to Mark's weekly telephone call and his next visit. It surprised her that the jolt each departure caused did not lessen as Mark grew older. Moira made herself concentrate as Ian began to talk. 'You think they were planted on the victims for your benefit? Seems a bit far-fetched, Ian. Besides, how many people know you support the team?' But it was odd because neither man had any connection with Norwich City. 'Maybe it was a sort of calling-card.'

Ian was staring vacantly in the direction of the window.

149

Outside was only blackness with the interior, domestic scene reflected in the panes of the glass, a little distorted but familiar. Some stray leaves slithered across the patio. Ian heard the ghostly rustle as they were blown up to the back door. They seemed to be enticing him out there. He shivered. He was not prone to fanciful ideas. Or was it his own brain telling him something? 'I think it could be a bit of both. I've got to make a phone call. Pour me a beer, will you, love?' The pre-dinner drink had long since become a ritual, and an enjoyable one, unless Ian was very late. It took place in the kitchen away from the distraction of the television which, Ian admitted, he tended to switch on indiscriminately. It gave them a chance to unwind, to adjust to each other again after the rigours of the day.

'Are you all right?' Moira asked when Ian returned with a concerned furrow creasing his brow.

'Mmm, I think so.' He no longer felt like talking. Instead he picked up his tankard and took a long swallow. 'Ah, nectar,' he said, smiling at Moira. The grin altered his entire face and took years off his age. He did not know that it always reminded Moira of what she had first seen in him. Later, when I'm asleep, he thought, my mind will fill in the gaps that're missing from my theory. '"An eye for an eye", that's what I think it is.' He had no idea why the biblical quote had suddenly come into his head.

'Everyone misquotes that. It's actually "eye for eye, tooth for tooth". Exodus. Look it up.' Moira, who had been a regular Sunday school-goer in her childhood and had in her early teens, like many other young girls, gone through a religious phase, could still quote freely from the Bible.

'I'll try and remember that.' Ian, beginning to relax and listening to Moira chatting as she prepared their meal, recalled what he had seen on one of the desks in the incident room which had prompted him to make the telephone call. It had been a few lines written in Markham's barely intelligible scrawl. The mind's a funny thing, he thought. I had no idea I'd read it and taken it in.

At ten o'clock he dialled Markham's home number and was relieved when he answered.

'Yes. I think we're right. I've left a note in Short's file,' he said when he had listened to the Chief for several minutes.

When the alarm clock shrilled in his ear the following morning Ian was awake instantly. He lay in bed wondering why this was so. It usually took ages for his head to clear and his body to respond to the messages from his brain dictating that it really was time to get up. Then he remembered the date.

Moira was already downstairs. Even in the winter she was an early riser. He could hear sounds from the kitchen and smelled the breakfast toast. He showered and shaved quickly and went to join her. It was not until he was buttering his second round of toast that his circuitous deliberations of last night fell into place. It was personal but he had been looking in the wrong direction. Not himself, not the police in general, but Markham and with a strong hint thrown in for good measure. 'Markham!' He jumped to his feet and pushed back his chair in one movement. It clattered against the cupboard beneath the worktop then righted itself.

'Ian?'

But he was already in the hall with the telephone in his hand. He should have warned him, he ought to have guessed what Markham would do. He was a one man crusade and he had to be stopped. 'Come on,' he told the ringing tone. 'Come on, answer me.' But Markham was not at home. He tried the station only to be told that the sergeant had been in earlier but had left again without saying where he was going.

'I think I know where he is. Listen, this is what I want you to do,' he told Inspector Short.

It had begun to sink into place last night for what he had noticed written on a sheet of paper was the date of the accident which had killed Martin Cooper. And now other things came crowding back. The scarf. The Norwich City scarf he had still been wearing when he had arrived back from the match in time to be the one to break the news to Andrews. How stupid he had been not to have seen it all before.

But Markham was a law unto himself and this was what worried Ian. He was going to have serious words with his detective sergeant.

Detective Inspector Short was rubbing his badly shaved cheek. He had followed the Chief's instructions to the letter and was now staring at the various bits of paper DC Campbell had handed him after he had asked Alan if he knew what the Chief was on

151

about. And now Markham, the bloody fool, was nowhere to be found when he was most needed. But if Markham had come to the same conclusion as the Chief then he would be expecting danger.

'But he can't have,' Short said aloud, 'or he would not be out there alone.'

'Sir?' Campbell's washed-out eyes regarded him with curiosity.

'Markham – has he talked about any of this with you?' Short rapped the papers in his hand.

'Not really. He's just asked me to find certain bits of information.'

'Which you didn't think it was necessary to share with your colleagues. What's happening to everyone? We're supposed to be a sodding team.'

Scarlet at the injustice of this chastisement Alan Campbell stood up to feel at less of a disadvantage. 'There's a copy of everything here on your desk, sir. It's been there since yesterday lunchtime and Sergeant Markham added some more information late last night. He assumed you'd already read the rest. And, with respect, sir, we are a team, it's just sometimes some of the players are missing.'

Short, chin almost on his chest, jowls between forefinger and thumb, looked up, glared at Alan then burst out laughing. 'Good for you, son. I didn't know you had it in you. And, yes, point taken.' He was hardly in a position to chide anyone when his own example was hardly exemplary. 'Did the Chief receive a copy?'

'No. It was assumed that you would discuss it with him.'

Dear, oh, dear, Short thought. Looks like it's going to be me on the Super's carpet, not Markham. At least he had acted in time. And now he had the unenviable task of talking to Danny Cotton. The hospital had told him that he would make a full recovery and that someone could see him that morning. Danny had spent the night in the company of a uniformed officer.

Short shrugged himself into his stained navy raincoat. He might as well get it over with and at the same time be out of the way when the Chief arrived. Ian's temper was not something to encounter first thing in the day. It was more bluster and frustration than anything personal and it soon evaporated, but avoidance was the preferable course of action if at all possible.

The sky had lightened at dawn but it had remained the same depressing grey ever since. At least the roads were dry and the traffic was now lighter as Short made his way to Rickenham General. The fingers of his stubby left hand tapped the wheel in time to the tune playing on Radio 2. As he whistled through his teeth he thought about Nancy. Nancy of the soft rounded limbs and the yeasty smell of femininity. It was time he went round there again. Tonight, he decided, whether or not he had been sacked. It was the perfect relationship. Now and then they'd go out for dinner but mostly it was bed. Not regularly, just when one or the other of them fancied it. Neither of them wanted permanency and sometimes it was as long as a fortnight before they met again. Oh, Nancy of the pendulous breasts and tousled hair, you have a big surprise coming to you tonight, he thought.

The spaces nearest the main hospital building had been filled a long time ago. Short had to drive right to the end of the car-park. It was mild enough not to have to button his raincoat and now a thin streak of yellowish white streaked the horizon with a hint of sunshine. Hands in his pockets, John Short strolled towards the entrance. There was no hurry, nothing in life was worth rushing for. Stepping inside he was greeted by the smell endemic to all such buildings; a mixture of things pleasant and unpleasant: almondy floor polish and antiseptic, the nurses' perfume and a sort of chalky-tea smell from behind the reception desk, the sweat of the cleaners in their nylon overalls, and fear. Short could detect that anywhere. It was common to police stations as well.

PC Cotton was in a side-room off a main ward. This was not preferential treatment, Miranda Ashton, the Sister, told him. She had thought it more prudent, for the sake of her other charges, not to have a uniformed copper smack in the middle of the ward where he would have inhibited the patients. In her experience conversation which flowed readily was as much of a tonic as any pills.

Short glanced at her name badge. Miranda smells delicious, he thought. Arpège, if I'm not mistaken. He had bought some for Nancy who dabbed it in places he had not thought women wore perfume. Miranda Ashton's skin was clear and ripe and spoke of a clean lifestyle because she was no youngster. Forty, forty-five? He couldn't tell as he followed her to Danny's room. Nice legs, hips on the fleshy side, just as he liked them. Straight dark hair pinned under her cap. Was it chin length or would it fall down her back when undone? He could picture it flowing over smooth, white shoulders. Must be the new regime, he thought. Can't get my mind off sex. Unbeknown to anyone he had been trying to eat more sensibly. Low calorie cereal had replaced the usual breakfast fry-up but it could never take the place of wiping the frying pan clean with a slice of bread and savouring the dark little bacon speckles which accumulated in the fat. And all because Nancy had squeezed his paunch playfully and made a joke at his expense. Well, he had lasted a couple of days and proved he could do it and that was enough. He was starving. Perhaps it was food he needed, not sex.

Sister Ashton opened the door and stood aside to allow Short to enter. She gave him a cursory but expert glance which took in the length of him from his scuffed shoes to the hair brushed thinly over his scalp then disappeared without a word.

No chance there, then, Short decided. 'Get yourself something in the canteen, son,' he told the PC who had been engrossed in a paperback. Any male who was ambulant without the aid of a walking frame merited the appellation of son to Short. 'I'll get Miranda to ring down when I've finished.' He spoke the name as if they had grown up together. 'How's it going, Danny?' He pulled the chair up to the bed until it was almost touching it.

Danny, pale as an arum lily, had a dead look in his eyes. He shrugged.

'Missus been to see you?'

'No.'

'Well, she's got a lot on her plate, with the kiddies.' Short squeezed his nostrils. 'Let's not pretend, eh? Why did you do it, Danny?'

Danny met his eyes, knowing that there was no way in which a man like Short, unkempt, uncaring and coarse, could ever understand what had driven him. He had wanted to possess Emma, to have her to himself completely. 'I love her.'

'Who? Emma Drew?'

'Yeah.'

'Funny way of showing it, son. Anything else we ought to know?'

'Such as?'

'Well, look at it from our point of view. You've got a family

154

and your wife's preggers again. You're pissed off because the conjugals are rationed or non-existent. You find something on the side, temporary, like, to see you through. It happens. It happens every single day but the world, being the sort of place it is, soon reverts back to normal once the baby's born or the girlfriend realises hubby isn't going to leave the wife for her. Mostly no one knows so no one gets hurt.

'But not in your case. Not only do you find yourself a woman, Danny, but you advertise the fact to the whole bloody town by holding her at knifepoint and threatening to do the pair of you in. You cannot fail to agree that that isn't normal or rational behaviour. It's the behaviour of a desperate man, and I'd like to know what drove him to it. I mean, people just don't go around acting like maniacs simply because of some little tart.' Despite Short's casual manner of speaking he had been watching Danny closely. Tart. The word had been used to provoke a reaction, to make Danny angry, angry enough to say too much, to give Short a clue as to Emma's association with Barbara Fletcher and, come to that, Danny's own relationship with the woman, because there was the little matter of two dead men and a house burglary to clear up as well as this latest fiasco. And they now knew that at the times of the murders Danny had been off duty. When Mrs Fletcher's house had been broken into, he had been at work and in that area. He possessed knowledge of the layout of the house and probably knew her regular movements.

He's not angry, Short realised, he's worried. He thought for a moment and then he realised why. 'I don't believe it.' Short's eyes shone but he was not laughing. Cotton was a bigger fool than he had taken him for. 'Don't tell me you really love her, you've really fallen for a Tom?'

'Get out,' Danny hissed as he reached up with a bandaged wrist for the bell with which to summon a nurse.

Short grabbed his fingers. 'You're already in a lot of trouble, son, don't make it worse for yourself. Just answer a few questions and I'll leave you alone. Where were you when De Quincy and Walters were killed? We've already spoken to your wife so we know you weren't at home.'

Danny sighed. He would have to go along with it. 'On the Saturday, with Emma. On Sunday I went out after lunch. I just walked, I needed to think.' Hadn't Jackie told them that he had offered to take two of the children? It had been bitterly cold, he had guessed she would say no, but that was irrelevant, he had offered.

That old chestnut. It was Short's turn to sigh. Strange how many of the criminal fraternity, not given to thinking about anything much at all, claimed they had found an urgent need to stretch their legs whilst they did a spot of philosophising just at the moment a crime was being committed. 'So you met Emma at the Fletcher woman's place?'

'Yes.' Danny felt on safer ground here. 'She was introduced to me as Barbara's niece. I know now that she isn't related.'

'Did you pay her any money, son? Give her any gifts?'

Danny's low laugh was cynical. 'How the hell could I afford to?'

Short believed him. What a top-grade idiot. How, then, did he suppose he was going to keep her and the wife and kiddies? The force would be better off without him although how he had got into it in the first place was beyond Short's comprehension. Fletcher had duped him because she had wanted the law on her side. Protection in reverse, almost. However, that could wait. 'Things got on top of you then?'

'You could say that.'

'Did you rob her, Mrs Fletcher? I mean, you knew the layout and what was there and you've admitted you're struggling.'

'I did not. I've been through all this with the DCI.'

Short chewed away at the limp straggly hair which grew down over his top lip. Was Cotton still a serious contender as a murder suspect? It was doubtful, even if he had threatened to kill both Emma and himself. He was immature and gullible and had probably mistaken lust for love – and, let's face it, he's thick, Short added. He had not had the sense to see that the affair was going nowhere, that a girl who worked all day then opened her legs for money was not going to settle for a life of poverty with a man who already had a family. And he had been even more stupid in believing he could keep her by threatening her. Would he have killed her if the woman downstairs had not called the police? They would never know. But he had certainly made a serious attempt on his own life. 'Richie Andrews, what do you know about him?' According to Markham, Danny had been asked to keep on eye on Andrews but had not reported in once.

An awful lot seemed to be going on on Cotton's patch that he didn't know about, And if what Markham and the Chief believed was true, then he must have been walking around with his eyes closed.

'Not much.' Danny hesitated. He had forgotten the man's existence. 'I know where he lives and I've seen him around. He seems harmless.'

My God, how did this one get through his induction course? Short wondered, realising he was wasting his time. He had no idea what would happen to Cotton, only that it was obvious he needed more than a physician to sort him out.

He tried to find Miranda Ashton on his way out, merely to ask her how long Danny was expected to stay in. The staff were trained in one-to-one nursing care for attempted suicides but Cotton had committed a crime, they could not take the risk of him discharging himself and disappearing into the sunset. On the other hand they could not leave a PC there for days on end. But Miranda Ashton was nowhere to be seen and he had to make do with the abrupt staff nurse who told him to ring back later when the consultant had done his rounds. But she smiled when he asked her to buzz the canteen and tell PC Hutchinson to come back up. So that's the way the land lies. Sex is certainly in the air this morning, Short decided as he waited for Hutchinson to return before he left the ward.

He was back at the car before the whirring cogs in his brain enmeshed. If, as they suspected, Barbara Fletcher was running a discreet little brothel, then she was open to blackmail in the same way as her clients were. But by the time he pulled out into the main road John Short saw there was no mileage in that idea. De Quincy certainly had the money to frequent the place and might well have popped back to do so, but Walters could not have afforded such a luxury. No, Barbara Fletcher, even if she knew someone willing to kill for her, had had no reason to wish for the disposal of both of the men. Only De Quincy. But just supposing De Quincy had been paying for Emma's services, how would Cotton have felt about that? He'd already shown how unstable he was.

Markham's theory seemed too flimsy and the motivation wrong. But then, killers sometimes had their own peculiar agenda.

Passing a parade of shops on the outskirts of Rickenham, Short pulled in on a single yellow line and went into a small café where he purchased a bacon roll. Saliva filled his mouth as he opened it and squirted a liberal amount of brown sauce over the contents. He ate as he drove, relishing every mouthful and ignoring the stickiness of the steering-wheel. He entered the police station unaware of the the sauce on his cheek and the crumbs clinging to his moustache.

Markham had left the station with the assumption that Short had read the file and the notes he had added, and made his way to Saxborough Road. He drove its length, surreptitiously glancing right and left as he did so, then returned via another route. Well done, Short, he thought, surprised he had taken him seriously and put a watch on the house. Markham had spotted two of the surveillance team and there might even be more. But Markham did not know it was the Chief who had arranged it and that Richie Andrews had already left the house before the team arrived.

He's bound to go to the grave, he had thought, before it occurred to him that someone like Richie Andrews would want to do so privately, would not want to run the risk of bumping into Cooper's parents. As indifferent as they might have been to their son in life, it was highly likely that they would pay their respects on the first anniversary of his death. So could Andrews have left the house early? He would have to return to the flat, they could tail him later.

The churchyard at St Luke's had been filled many years ago and the land set aside for the cemetery lay some distance away. Markham drove towards it. It was surrounded by high railings and there was a separate section which housed the crematorium and its memorial gardens. The older part held family vaults with crumbling angels and elaborate graves, their marble surrounds covered in loose chippings. The newer side was comprised of small plots with simple headstones, their engraving still legible. It was where Martin Cooper lay.

Markham cruised around the perimeter and grinned. In the distance he saw the thin figure of Andrews standing with his hand resting on a headstone. Driving further down the road out of sight, he informed headquarters and said he was on his way back. Even Markham knew that he could not be the one to tail Richie. The plan was that it should be the other way around.

Richie had entered the locked cemetery by standing on the back of the metal seat at the bus-stop and levering himself over the spiked railings. Dew dampened the leather uppers of his shoes and he breathed in the clean smell of crushed grass and damp soil as he walked.

Standing by the grave of the only person who had cared about him Richie felt the full desolation of his loss again. 'I'll get him,' he promised. 'I'll get him for you.'

He felt awkward and confused. Alone, he communicated with Martin every day, yet now, in the cemetery, there seemed nothing left to say. His throat ached with unshed tears. 'I miss you, you bastard,' he whispered and thumped the granite headstone with the heel of his hand. He left then, feeling traitorous for leaving Martin there alone without even Johnny Vaughan for company. Johnny had been cremated.

He retrieved his hold-all from beneath a bush and left through the main gates which were now open.

'Thank God. Where've you been?' were the Chief's words of greeting when Markham returned.

'Paying my respects to the dead.'

'We'll pick him up. His place is being watched.' But just then the phone rang. The car that had been sent to the cemetery got there too late. There had been no sign of Richie Andrews. 'Okay, Markham, this is how we play it. If you're right, and I think you are, you'll be shadowed all day. If it's you he wants then today's the day.'

They discussed it for an hour, along with DC Gibbons and DC Campbell. Ian thought he saw the reason for the two deaths. De Quincy, whose crime was minimal, paid for it with his life in return for Vaughan's life, because, in Andrews' eyes, Vaughan had been minimal. Walters had killed a child, had robbed a family of the thing they loved best, just as Andrews had been robbed. He had died for it.

159

But it was Markham who had been driving the pursuit car, Markham who had passed all the necessary tests to be able to so, and in Richie Andrews' eyes, Markham had killed his friend.

'So you're the bait,' Brenda commented. Markham did not seem overly concerned that someone wanted to kill him, but it was hard to know what did concern him.

By lunchtime there was still no sighting of Andrews. 'He must know we're on to him,' Short commented. 'He's skipped.'

'No,' Ian said. 'I don't think he has.' So, while Markham was out in the streets, carefully watched by fellow officers, they waited.

Brenda and Alan were sent to have a word with Barbara Fletcher. Emma Drew had already left.

'Emma? She's a friend,' Barbara told them, hoping she was wrong about their reason for wanting to know. 'A close friend,' she added.

'And Police Constable Cotton?'

'A pleasant young man who keeps an eye on us all around here.'

'But you introduced them?' Alan persisted.

'Yes. Emma happened to be here on one occasion when he called in. I'm sure you'd hardly class that as a crime. I had absolutely no idea they were seeing each other.' Emma would have to stand on her own in that regard.

'So your close friend didn't confide in you?'

'I expect she was protecting him. I believe he's married. The poor girl. Danny's obviously had some sort of breakdown to have done such a thing.'

Tactfully they inquired about other visitors to the house but Barbara managed to brush off their questions with innocent replies.

'Well, as you've been broken into once, we'll be keeping a closer watch from now on.'

'How very kind of you. Now, I really must ask you to leave. I've got a busy day ahead of me.'

They left but they knew they had been right and they knew that Mrs Fletcher knew. 'She won't risk it again,' Brenda commented.

'Odd about that burglary, though. She doesn't seem that bothered that we haven't got anybody for it.' Alan wondered if she, as they had done, thought Danny Cotton was responsible and did not want to look a fool for having made a house guest of him.

'I think we'll take a little look into her background,' Ian decided, when he heard what they had to say. 'Just a few basic inquiries. Find out where she came from and who she is.'

By mid-afternoon they had more information than they had bargained for, but what they had learned only added to the confusion. Barbara Fletcher had once been married to Norman Andrews, a man much older than herself who had met her through a mutual friend. They could only conjecture at her past before that time, but their suspicions seemed the logical answer. Norman Andrews had provided her with a way out of that kind of life even if he had been unaware she was living it. And they had had a son. Richard Andrews.

'Bring her in,' Ian said.

Barbara Fletcher's veneer of confidence left her immediately she was shown into an interview room. How different it was from her own, comfortable, elegant lounge, and the grim faces of Inspector Short and Constable Gibbons did nothing to alleviate her fears. But the first question surprised her.

'We believe you have a son, Richard, Mrs Fletcher?'

'I . . .' She hesitated. 'I did have. We have had no contact since he was a boy.'

'I find that hard to believe,' Short continued, 'since he lives here in Rickenham Green and not all that far from you. Fletcher's your maiden name?'

'Yes. I reverted to it after my divorce.' Barbara realised that lying would do her no good. They had already looked into her background, she did not want them to make further inquiries. 'I did see Richard,' she admitted. 'But I wasn't sure what he wanted from me. He came to the house. I didn't recognise him because I hadn't seen him since he was a small boy. He looked ill to me.' She paused, recalling her inadequacy in dealing with the situation.

'How did he know where to find you?'

'His father had written to him giving him my address. I can only imagine he did so because he had reached the age of twenty-one

161

and he had decided it was up to Richard now if he wanted to see me. Richard lived in London then. Apparently, my being here prompted him to move. Or so he said.

'However, he didn't make contact right away, not for some months, although he didn't say why not.' It struck Barbara that her son might have been watching her for some time before that day when he rang her bell, might even know what went on in Saxborough Road. 'When he did turn up he told me his best friend had died. I think,' she added thoughtfully, 'that he was somehow expecting me to fill the gap.'

And you let him down yet again, Short thought, pulling at his moustache.

'So your husband knew where you lived?'

'Yes. When I left he set me up in a house in Surrey. We had no further contact but I felt it polite to let him know I'd moved. I simply sent a change of address card.' Too late, she wished she had not. It had unsettled her far more than she expected when Richard had turned up. She did not love him, had, in fact, never loved him. An inbuilt terror of rejection always prevented her from getting close to people and she had ended up perpetuating the ways of her own parents, thus damaging others.

Is it true that I don't love him? Barbara wondered. It was the first time she had given the matter real thought. There had been times when he was little when she would have liked to stroke his silky head but she had recoiled from such gestures.

She had not realised that Richard was still around. Not until she had thought long and hard about the burglary did she suspect her son might have been responsible. Who else would have taken the china ballerina with her faded, shabby net tutu which her mother had won at a fairground and brought back for her? It was worthless but she had loved it for what it was and because it was one of the few gifts she had ever received, apart from in the course of her work. And the silver snuff-box which had been her grandfather's, given to her by him because he knew his own son would have sold it. No doubt it had some value now but not a great deal. The rest, the money and the real valuables, meant nothing and could be replaced. This was the reason for the questioning, she realised. They had worked it out and thought she was protecting her son. She wasn't. She had only just worked out the possibility herself and it still could be that the thief was a stranger who had taken things at random, the things closest to hand, and did not know the difference between clay and porcelain.

'Do you know where your son is now?'

'No. I've no idea.'

'He hasn't been to see you recently?'

'No.' It was not a lie. If Richard had broken in, she had not been there to see him. But they still had not mentioned the burglary. 'Why is any of this important?'

'Mrs Fletcher, what do you know about Richard?'

'Very little. He lived with his father from the time he was seven. I know he had a university place which he didn't take and that he moved to London. He came to see me here just once, that was all. He mentioned that his father still pays him an allowance, although God knows why, he's old enough to earn his own living.' She bit her lip at the uncomfortable memory which reflected badly upon her own character. On that single visit she had assumed that Richard had found out what was going on and had come to blackmail her for his silence. It had not been money he wanted, but love. He had moved here to be near her even if he hadn't had the courage to see her at once. Could she have prevented him mixing with criminals if he'd come to her immediately? No, she realised with sadness. I would have turned him away under any circumstances.

Brenda and John Short looked at each other. Mrs Fletcher had said nothing about her son's involvement in the crime which had ended with the deaths of two young men. Richie had said his friend was dead but it seemed as if he had failed to mention the surrounding conditions.

'Do you take the *Rickenham Herald*, Mrs Fletcher?' Brenda continued.

'No.' Barbara thought the question odd but the young woman must have had a reason for asking it.

'Did your son tell you how Martin Cooper died?'

'No. I didn't even know the boy's name. I assumed it was from some awful illness.' Patting her hair nervously, she wondered what on earth could be coming next. Surely Richard hadn't killed him?

John Short explained briefly. As unlikely as it seemed, Mrs Fletcher reacted with genuine surprise. She said she took no interest in local news and, on reflection, Short recalled that it had been Cooper and Vaughan whose names had made the tragic headlines. Probably the article had run along the lines of a third man helping with their inquiries, and later, Richie's court appearance would only have warranted a few lines somewhere inside the paper. It was a first offence and he didn't try to run, he was given a suspended sentence.

'Mrs Fletcher, we're trying to trace Richard because we believe he may be able to help us in connection with some cases we're dealing with.'

Barbara smiled at Brenda. She was right, it was the burglary. Well, the least she could do for Richard now was to help to keep him out of further trouble. She supposed she owed him at least that much. 'You think he broke into my house?'

No, we didn't think that, Brenda said silently, avoiding meeting Short's eyes because it had not crossed anyone's mind. But now you mention it, it seems quite likely. The woman had rejected him again. If their assessment of his psychology was correct, she, too, would have had to be punished. But Mrs Fletcher had turned very pale. Judging that she had nothing further to tell them, they decided to let her go. 'If he should try to contact you in any way, we'd be grateful if you'd let us know at once,' Short said, standing up to indicate that the interview was at an end.

'Of course.' Barbara also got to her feet. Richard won't come back now, she thought.

Immediately she reached home she rang several estate agents and made appointments for them to come and value the house. There was no way now she could possibly remain in Rickenham Green.

Several times during the course of the afternoon Markham returned to the station. He was bored more than worried.

Andrews had not returned to the flat. They had obtained a search warrant but it had proved to be a waste of time. If any clothes were missing they did not know it and nothing incriminating had been found. The newspapers were there which contained the reports on the hearings but so were many others and the articles had not been ringed or underlined.

'What now?' Markham said as he drank a cup of coffee.

'We keep trying. He's out there somewhere,' Ian said philosophically.

It was nine thirty when Ian decided enough was enough. Markham was to drive straight home. He would be followed rather than have someone in the car with him in case Andrews was waiting for him near his flat. They needed to find him, but it would be neater if they did so as he was about to make an attempt on Markham's life.

Markham's headlights picked out the dustbins in the area behind the building in which he lived. The flat was over a shop and the way in was up the fire escape at the back. He swung the car around to make sure there was no one lurking in the yard then parked.

His footsteps rang on the the metal gangway. He inserted his key in the simple Yale lock, pushed the door open quietly and listened. There was only silence. Quickly he moved through the rooms throwing on switches. His radio was in his hand, the line open. 'It's okay,' he said into it, surprised at the relief he felt. He had not realised quite how nervous he had been. 'We'll be here all night,' the disembodied voice told him.

He locked the door and drew the curtains. It was doubtful if he would sleep in case Andrews broke in and took him by surprise despite the men posted outside.

He wasn't hungry but he felt like a drink. Just the one, his head must stay clear. There was some lager in the fridge. He went to get it.

12

They were eating a late meal of beef stew which Moira had had the foresight to prepare because there was no telling when Ian might get home and stew did not spoil. 'What is it, Ian?' she asked, recognising the troubled expression on his face.

He tried to explain, but, as Short had thought earlier, it all sounded rather tenuous, as if they were clutching at straws.

'Where is he now, Markham?' she asked, biting into a carrot.

'At home. There're men outside.'

'Poor Markham. I bet he won't sleep tonight. Are you sure this Andrews person hasn't just gone away?' She paused. 'Ian, you don't know for certain that he killed those two men, do you?'

'No. I don't. But I want it to be him. I want this to be sorted out. There's nowhere else to turn.'

'Odd that, about his mother. Was that why he came here?'

'It looks that way, but it took some time before he had the nerve to visit her. She doesn't want to know, apparently, no wonder he's a mess. Apart from Cooper he's never had anyone he could turn to. His mother was a last resort but she let him down again.'

Moira couldn't understand it. The idea of turning Mark away made her feel sick. 'He wouldn't have gone running to the father, by any chance?'

Ian, slumped at the table, shook his head. 'No. We spoke to him earlier. He remarried some time ago.' Norman Andrews had spoken quite honestly about his previous marriage. 'My wife had no feelings, chief inspector. She cared little for me and nothing for the boy. I'm afraid I didn't handle him very well either. He came to me late in life, perhaps I was just too old, and my second wife showed no interest in Richard. I wish now that I'd spent more time with him. However, it's too late for regrets. I'll ring you immediately if I hear from him.'

They sat in silence over their coffee which Ian had said he wanted even though it was late. He doubted if he would sleep much either.

'Go on, ring,' Moira said as they were going up to bed a little before midnight. Ian had been eyeing the telephone. 'If you're right, if today's so important, he'd have to do it today.'

Ian lifted the receiver and rang the station. There had been no sighting of Andrews and all was quiet. According to the men on watch, Markham had gone straight in and switched on all the lights then reported everything was all right. He was presumably still up because all the lights had remained on. 'Thanks,' Ian said, and smiled with relief. It was five past twelve.

Half-way up the stairs he stopped. All the lights were still on. He had had that serious word with Markham and had underlined the importance of someone being with him all day; he had also stressed that he must act as naturally as possible to prevent Andrews from becoming suspicious. Was it Markham's practice to leave every room illuminated when he was at home? Markham was what Ian's father would once have termed one of the awkward squad. If he was more worried about Andrews than he was letting on Markham would have done the opposite, he'd have sat in the dark and tried to draw him in.

Ian went back downstairs and dialled his number. There was no reply. For a few minutes the discipline of training was ascendant over emotion. He rang the station again and issued his instructions rapidly. 'I'm going out,' he shouted up the stairs to Moira.

The front door slammed loudly before she could stick her head around the bathroom door to reply.

Richie had followed Markham home on several occasions to make certain it was where he lived rather than a friend's place he was visiting. His plan was unbelievably simple and it had worked so easily. He had decided to get into Markham's flat and wait for him there. He would be alone, he was always alone, and there were no signs that the police were on to him. It was farcical, he had to admit it, but he guessed that Markham, knowing what the date was, might make a search of the flat before settling down. But he did not look in the cupboard in the hall where some of his shoes were kept along with a clutter of buckets and domestic cleaning things.

Richie had stiffened when he heard him speak, imagining that he was wrong, that for once Markham had company, until he realised he was on the phone. 'It's okay,' he had said. And that meant they did know, that there were people outside waiting to catch him. He had to act quickly.

When he heard the fridge door open he stepped out of the cupboard soundlessly. The knife was already in his hand. 'Not much of a door lock for a policeman's pad,' he said from the kitchen doorway.

Markham spun round and saw the knife. There was nothing within his reach he could use as a weapon and his phone was on the settee in the living-room. It was a long time since he had had to disarm a man and then there had been two of them to do it.

He had not expected Andrews to come here; he had imagined that his death or an attempt on his life would take place out of doors, maybe in some dark alley. But why? Just because that was the way it had been for De Quincy and Walters.

'You killed Martin. You were driving the car chasing him.'

There was no point in arguing or trying to reason with him. Nor was there any point in asking him what he wanted. He knew the answer to that. Markham turned very slowly and picked up the can of lager. It was open. Throwing it in Andrews' face would cause a distraction and give him vital seconds to make it out on to the fire escape.

But Richie's eyes had flickered to where his hand was going. He lunged forward, thrusting the knife upwards.

When Markham smiled Richie saw that they were two of a kind, that neither of them had much to live for and that the man whose breath was upon his face had somehow won.

Pictures of his parents, both dead, and his own life flashed through Markham's mind. What was he? What had he achieved? Had his life been worthwhile? None of it seemed to matter any more. His life had really ended when Julie died.

There was no pain at first, only a warm feeling when the knife was pulled out and the blood started to flow. When it penetrated a second time he conceded that he had underestimated Richie Andrews and that he really was going to die. He could not be bothered to put up a fight.

By the time the men watching from the street had been alerted that there was no reply from Markham's telephone, Richie Andrews had climbed the fire escape to the second floor and edged his way along the cast-iron guttering with his body flat to the roof. At the end of the row of shops, dizzy and sick with vertigo, he had managed to get down to the ground by way of a drainpipe. He was in another yard but this one was enclosed. In the darkness he sought out an exit. Rubbish was stacked in front of a gate with a rusty bolt. Once it was open he found himself in an alley and continued walking away from the direction of Markham's flat. He did not think himself safe yet. He had no idea how many men would be looking out for him. But they wouldn't expect to find him back in Saxborough Road. That was the last place they'd think of looking. And they didn't know about Barbara Fletcher. His mother.

Ian stood on the small landing of the fire escape and stared at the scene in Markham's kitchen. His throat constricted with horror. He wanted to shout with anger and outrage. It wasn't possible. It just couldn't be true. Not Markham. Campbell or Short or himself, yes, but Markham had always struck them as indestructible. It shouldn't be like this, he thought, it shouldn't be worse because it's one of our own. But it was. His words to Moira came back to him. You didn't believe it could happen to someone you know. Seeing Markham lying there, his blood spilled across the kitchen floor, made Ian see his own life in a new perspective. How ridiculous and petty his anxiety about slowing down and getting old seemed by comparison. Life was precious, every day should be lived to the full.

'He's dead, sir.'

Ian nodded. There was nothing he could say, nothing he wanted to say. And all the time he blamed himself. There should have been someone with him. In the room with him the whole time.

His radio came to life. 'Yes?'

'We've spotted him. He's on foot, heading east along Saxborough Road.' It was Short, Short who had stayed on at the station, who had decided against seeing Nancy because the more he thought about it the more he knew that Markham really was in danger and he was determined to stick it out until midnight.

He already had his coat on when Ian's call came in at 00.06. And he had done what he was so good at. He had outguessed Richard Andrews. It was too late for Markham, but not for Barbara Fletcher.

Short flung himself from the car just as Andrews rang the bell at number 101. A light came on upstairs. As Barbara Fletcher opened the door on the chain Short grabbed Richie and twisted his arm behind his back, jerking it with far more force than was necessary. 'I hope I've fucking broken it,' he hissed as Richie screamed in pain.

'Stay inside,' he told Barbara, 'and don't open the door until we tell you to.'

169

With assistance he got Richie into the car. His face was white but he no longer struggled. He sat in the back of the car between two officers, handcuffed to the one on his right. Short got into the driving seat; he did not trust himself not to do further damage to Andrews and to hell with the consequences. Mrs Fletcher did not know how lucky she was. Had she let her son in, he would have killed her too.

When it was over, when the procedure for murder – which had been no different even though the victim was Markham – had been followed, Ian went back to headquarters. He did not want to interview Andrews, he could not bear to do so. That job was allocated to someone else, someone who had not known Markham as well as his own team.

He was still there when DCs Campbell and Gibbons arrived within minutes of each other in the morning. 'In here, Brenda,' he said quietly, leading her into an empty room. 'I'll be back in a minute.'

Then Alan appeared and he and Ian joined Brenda.

Ian lit a cigarette as he stood directly beneath the No Smoking sign, then he rubbed his head. 'There's no easy way to say this,' he began.

Brenda swallowed and looked down at her feet. She knew what was coming. I'm going to cry, she thought. And she did. When she looked up she saw that the Chief wasn't far from it himself and Alan was blowing his nose.

Ian had not expected to feel so very much. When you worked with people, when you were constantly in their company, you tended to take them for granted. Markham was Markham, that's how they'd seen him. Unorthodox, enigmatic, often silent, good at what he did, but always there. He was a man they had felt they knew yet they had hardly known him at all. Ian wished he had made time to draw him out rather than simply accept the persona he presented. Now they would never know what had gone on beneath the surface.

They sat in the silent room, each with their own thoughts. Superintendent Thorne was on his way to see them. He would deal with the media, he had said, and with Markham's relatives, if any could be traced. There was no next-of-kin listed in his personnel file.

Brenda was taking it badly. Markham had never done her a bad turn and he had treated her with more respect than some of her male colleagues. And there had been moments, she knew, when she had come as close to the man as he permitted anyone to come. And now he was dead.

Thorne entered the room quietly. He was not unmoved himself but he controlled his voice and hoped they found his words, spoken in the now familiar Birmingham accent, of some help. 'I think it would be best if you all went home. Andrews will be dealt with according to the law and I expect you to treat the case with the same degree of professionalism and lack of bias as any other.

'You have lost a colleague, possibly a friend, but we cannot give up because of this. I know it isn't much consolation, but you did manage to save a fourth victim.' He glanced around the room. 'Where's Inspector Short?'

Brenda bowed her head and sobbed into the palms of her hands. That one phrase, that so often repeated question, had opened the floodgates. Markham was no longer here but everything else would continue the same as before. I liked him, she thought. I know we weren't close, but I really did. Like Ian, she regretted not knowing him better.

'Nothing's ever going to be the same again,' Alan said. 'Nothing.'

'Nothing ever can be when something like this happens,' Mike Thorne said. 'Our job now is to try to make sure it never happens again.' But as he left he knew it would be a very long time before the other three people in the room came to terms with it. There would be constant reminders of Markham and many moments of soul-searching when they would wonder if they could have prevented his death. Had Markham, whose history he knew even if his colleagues weren't aware of it, welcomed that knife in much the same way as Walters had probably done? Superintendent Thorne did not believe in an afterlife, but he hoped that Markham had done so because he would also have had to believe that Julie Langdon, the girl he had hoped to marry, would be there waiting for him.

Thorne was being realistic rather than callous in recognising that the furore over not finding Andrews sooner would be tempered by the fact that a policeman had lost his life in the line of duty, in the very act of seeking him out. Such a fact would lessen his superiors' anger at their slowness and appease the public demand for action.

Barbara Fletcher was stunned when the police returned in the morning to break the news of her son's arrest.

'He's asked to see you.'

'What for? I thought you said he wanted to kill me.'

'He wants to talk to you.'

'Then will you tell him I'm sorry, but it's out of the question.'

The minute they had left she rang one of the estate agents and offered him the sole agency if he could find a quick buyer. She also reduced her asking price. Never before had the standing invitation from her friend in Bangor seemed so appealing. She would go and stay with her until the house was sold. The agent was coming to collect a spare key and would deal with all the arrangements. It was time to move on.

Elizabeth Smith heard the news as she was boiling an egg for breakfast. She frowned. Detective Sergeant Markham had been the man who had come to her house. He was dead.

She was no longer hungry and her hand shook as she poured her tea. She had lied. She had lied about the moustache, she hadn't seen that man's face. Was she in some way to blame? Had Sergeant Markham not realised he was in danger because he was expecting a man with a moustache to come after him?

Elizabeth went to the table by the window and picked up her notepad in which she jotted the comings and goings in Alma Road. She took it out to the kitchen and, page by page, tore it up, stuffing the pieces firmly in amongst the tea-leaves and rubbish in the bin.

At Rickenham Green headquarters the shock waves took a long time to recede. Ian's only consolation was at the funeral a fortnight later when a surprisingly large number of people came to acknowledge the death of Markham, loner though he had been. Martin Cooper, another loner, had had only four people to acknowledge his death. Apart from the team there were the usual police representatives, the braid brigade as they were known, and, surprisingly, members of the general public. Through her tears Brenda Gibbons pointed out Elizabeth Smith and someone else commented upon an old lady from Magnolia House, an eyesore of a building with more than its fair share of crime and criminals. 'He got her wedding ring back for her, sir, whilst he was working on another case,' a vaguely familiar face told him.

Oh, Markham, Ian thought, all these people, some of them strangers to me. They liked you. They probably saw a side of you I didn't know existed.

When it was over Ian stood at the graveside. Superintendent Thorne had arranged a bit of a do in the social club. There were no relatives so it had seemed the least he could do. They'd all be there and they'd all drink too much but that was the way things were done. Ian felt a hand on his arm. He looked down. A wizened old lady stood at his side. It was the lady who had been pointed out to him. 'You won't remember me,' she said. 'My name's Mrs Bennett. I live at Magnolia House. You came to see me once. I knew Sergeant Markham. Not well, you understand, but well enough to know what he was.' Ian nodded. 'He was not what he appeared, you know. He had something that is rare today. He had compassion.'

'Mrs Bennett . . .' Ian choked on the words, but she had already started to limp away. I want to know, he said to himself. I want to know the man that was Markham. But it was too late. He leant against the trunk of a tree feeling overwhelmed with sadness.

Moira Roper watched her husband carefully. She could see what he was going through. Not only had he lost an officer, but he felt responsible for his death. He had taken the news of Barry Swan's decision to leave the area badly; Markham's death had shaken him to the core.

'He was always true to his principles and life seems a little less without him, somehow,' Ian commented one evening when he was finally prepared to talk about what had happened.

173

There was nothing Moira could say. Now, with tulips and aconites in bloom and the hope of rebirth embodied by another spring, it might be possible for Ian to forgive himself. For that was the root of his trouble, she knew that even if he didn't.

Their holiday was less than two weeks away. Ian had said it was up to her where they went and left her to make all the arrangements. They were going to Scotland where they would take long walks and eat plenty of good food. But for the first night, the Saturday night, she had booked an hotel in Norwich. She was taking him to the match. By subtle means she had discovered they were playing at home. He did not know it yet and she was uncertain of his reaction but she would insist upon it whatever he said.

On the morning after Markham had died he had come home and folded up his Norwich City scarf and shoved it at the back of his sock drawer. It had stayed there ever since and Ian had refused to go to any of the games.

She sighed. How ironical it was that right at the beginning of it all she had cried because she thought that Ian might be dead. It's Markham who's dead, but my husband isn't fully alive, she realised. I want him back, she decided. I don't want this guilt-ridden creature as a husband. And with that thought she went to the bedroom and yanked open his sock drawer.

At six thirty Ian walked through the kitchen door of 14 Belmont Terrace, kissed his wife absent-mindedly and went to hang his jacket in the hall. If he had seen his Canaries scarf hanging on the hook he said nothing but there was a slight twitching around the corners of his mouth as if he had found something amusing.

Moira poured their drinks and placed them on the table. 'What is it, Ian? You've got an odd expression on your face.'

He met her eyes. 'You can't fool me, but they're away on Saturday.'

'But not the Saturday after,' Moira replied decisively. 'There's to be no argument. I'm even coming with you.'

'My God!' But Ian was smiling.

'Only this once,' she added hastily. Wondering at the wisdom of her idea she took a large sip of her wine.